Ghosts of the Tsunami
and Other Dark Tales (Vol. 1-3)

Walk beside everyday people who take an unexpected look into the shadows in these 13 tales with a supernatural twist.

Ghosts of the Tsunami An emergency dispatcher makes a fateful decision when a tsunami is about to strike and is haunted by the consequences.

Aunt Olga and the Werewolf With an injured werewolf roaming the mountains, no one is safe. Least of all elderly Aunt Olga, who refuses to move closer to town with her goats. Will Sandor and his cousins be able to keep her safe at the next full moon?

The Incident at Deep Lake When a hunter obsessed with a remote lake accidentally shoots a professor on vacation, he holds him captive and refuses to leave the lake. Is it madness, or is something really hiding in the deep water?

Hell Couch "We need a couch," Kellie tells her boyfriend. The two students are so broke when they move in together that they buy a used couch ... that turns out to have a horrifying secret hidden under the old cushions.

... and nine more dark stories from the swamps of Louisiana to the streets of Manhattan

Cover design by The Cover Collection
www.thecovercollection.com

Book design by Polgarus Studio
www.polgarusstudio.com

Ghosts of the Tsunami and Other Dark Tales (Vol. 1-3)
© 2016 AC Stone, KM Rockwood, BG House, and HA Grant

This collection includes:
The Wreck of U-913 and Other Dark Tales (Vol. 2)
© 2015 AC Stone, KM Rockwood, BG House, and HA Grant
Swamp Mansion and Other Dark Tales (Vol. 1)
© 2014 AC Stone, KM Rockwood, BG House, and HA Grant

ISBN Print Edition
ISBN-13: 978-1533625588
ISBN-10: 1533625581

Contents

Ghosts of the Tsunami and Other Dark Tales (Vol. 3)

Ghosts of the Tsunami
AC Stone

Exactly one year ago tonight, thirteen people drowned at Cedar Cliff Campground, and if I'd made that one decision differently, they'd be alive today.

I've tried to stop thinking about it. I really have, but I can't. I can still see everything that happened that evening clearly in my mind.

A magnitude 6.7 earthquake hit without warning ninety miles off the southern coast of Oregon. Our brick fire station rattled violently as shockwaves slammed into Ambrose, our small town. A quake measuring 6.7 might not sound all that powerful, but the shaking walls and swinging fluorescent lights sent half the firefighters of Company 3 bolting from their chairs and onto our concrete driveway. We had just started to tease the guys who ran out like scared baby chickens when the switchboard lit up with 911 calls. I raced back to my desk in the Communications Center.

Panicked locals called in to find out what happened. Folks reported that the disaster had darkened traffic lights from Main Street all the way to Carson Avenue. I had a good view of the town from the huge windows on the second floor. The violent tremors toppled some utility poles. Overloaded transformers crackled and buzzed as glowing blue sparks burst outwards and drifted toward the ground. Sagging black powerlines hung across roadways.

3

Most of the rural fishing villages from Ophir down to Gold Beach also lost electricity. The generator at our fire station kicked in immediately, keeping our lights and computers going, but power outages shrouded the rest of Ambrose in an eerie stillness.

The 911 dispatcher took calls for two different traffic accidents, including an overturned vehicle. I hoped the sheriff wouldn't call for medical transport for both accidents at the same time, because Company 3 had only one ambulance. The next fire station was twenty-five miles away and busy with its own emergencies. As the firefighters grabbed their coats and gear, the paramedics waited for me to tell them who needed the ambulance more urgently. It was going to be a long night.

Truth be told, I have always been envious of the firefighters as they charged out to fires and other emergencies. Don't get me wrong, I liked working with them from the Communications Center – the connection point between the 911 operators, the Sheriff's Department, and our teams. If I could've passed the physical exams, I'd have been a police officer or a firefighter somewhere along the scenic rocky coast of Oregon, but that wasn't meant to be. A congenital defect on my left leg required a prosthetic, which nobody could really notice under my pant leg, but it limited my career options. I did what I could, keeping the communications between our teams running efficiently.

Lights flashed across my panels as the 911 operators forwarded multiple reports to me, which I prioritized by type and location. I sent our ambulance to the overturned pick-up truck on State Road 216. Debbie Ortega came through the door to the Communications Center not a minute too soon, her shiny black hair out of place as if she had just woken up.

"Hey, what're you doing here?" I asked her, very much relieved.

"Figured you'd need the help, Peter. Folks from the other shifts are headin' in, as well."

"You're right ... and thanks."

Debbie dragged an office chair over to my desk where she also worked, but always on a different shift. She plunked down next to me.

"Did you see this message from the U.S. Geologic Survey?" she asked, pointing at my overloaded screen.

"Yeah, aftershocks. Next three days."

"Usually the first quake is the most intense. Aftershocks, not so much."

Just when we started on the rest of the calls, the urgent alert from the National Oceanic and Atmospheric Administration appeared on my computer screen. The worst of the night was about to arrive.

A twenty-foot tsunami would slam into southern Oregon in forty-five to sixty minutes. Tall cliffs protected most of the towns along the coast, but not all of them. I forwarded the tsunami warning to everyone in Company 3 so we could evacuate the villages on the shoreline.

"Good God," Debbie whispered gravely, almost like an uncertain prayer.

The Emergency Alert System had already connected with the local television and radio stations. I pinged an emergency message to the local police departments, town mayors, and county commissioners. Then I sent a mass email and texted everyone who had signed up for the Curry County alert system. Leaving Debbie to handle the 911 dispatch orders, I spread the message on social media. Everyone had to get as far away from the coastline as fast as possible.

I just shook my head as I flipped through the three-ring binder of protocols. I had taken all the steps required by the book. Debbie double-checked me, which I didn't mind under the circumstances.

She said, "You got it all. Now you take over the 911s."

Then it dawned on me. Cedar Cliff Campground was just off the beach. A twenty-foot wall of water was heading straight there. We'd scheduled a meeting next Wednesday with the elderly owners to connect the campground to the county alert system, but that wasn't going to help us now. Those campers were in real danger.

"Debbie, stay on the board."

"Got it," she said.

I frantically searched the internet for the phone number of the campground.

"Cedar Cliff is in a bad cell," I explained. "They're just off the beach underneath those giant stone bluffs where there's no reception. Unless someone there heard the EAS alert over the radio or TV, they don't know about the tsunami."

I yanked the phone receiver from its cradle and dialed the number, but a recording from Pacific Bell cheerfully explained, "We're sorry, but all circuits are busy. Please try your call again later."

I slammed the receiver down harder than I intended. My cellphone didn't work either. The call went straight to voicemail. There was just no reception out there.

"Nothing?" Debbie asked as she turned away from the communications panel.

"Nope."

"Email them. It's something."

I linked to the website for Cedar Cliff Campground, searched for an email address, and found it under the "Contact Us" button. A camping reservation form appeared on my screen. The email address read "info@cedarcliffcampground." I sent a quick message, but had no confidence anyone would get it in time. I'd been to Cedar Cliff, and they encouraged campers to turn off their electronic devices and experience nature without distractions. We'd wasted ten minutes trying to reach them, while at the same time Debbie and I relayed messages from the 911 operators to our teams in the field. I studied the current locations of our fire engine, the ambulance, and the sheriff's patrol cars on the GPS tracking board.

Debbie had to be thinking the same as I was and asked, "Who's close by?"

"No one," I replied. "The engine is responding to a ruptured gas line in Culbert. The ambulance is on route to the hospital. The sheriff's deputies are evacuating neighborhoods out there." I pointed to the string of fishing villages several miles north of Cedar Cliff Campground. No one was free to warn the campers.

Debbie nervously tapped a ballpoint pen on the edge of her keyboard.

I said, "There's no way to reach them."

"We just had an earthquake. Maybe they turned on the television."

"Yeah, maybe. But what if they lost power? Would they even think about a tsunami?" I looked at the analog clock on the wall, its red second hand swinging quickly around the numbers. A cold drip of perspiration travelled down my back. My damp shirt collar felt tight and itchy.

"You gotta work the board alone," I said to Debbie.

She lifted an eyebrow and stared at me with confused eyes.

I said, "I'm goin' out there and warn them."

"Go," she said without hesitation.

I sprinted to my Jeep, or at least what I considered a sprint on my bad leg. When I had to, I could move fast, but only in short bursts. I climbed into the driver's seat and briefly fumbled with my keys – perhaps from adrenaline, nerves, or just going out on a call for the first time. I fired up the ignition.

Cedar Cliff Campground was only twenty minutes away down the Coastal Highway, a long and winding strip of asphalt that hugged the beach just above sea level. I approached the fork in the road where Coastal Highway split off to Route 394, the southern pass through the foothills of the Oregon Coast Range. If the giant wave hit earlier than expected, I couldn't handle it. A twenty-foot wall of water crashing onto Coastal Highway would hurtle my Jeep onto the rocks, trapping me inside. I guess I always had to think differently from other people. The direct route made more sense, but to be honest, I wasn't all that strong and not much of a swimmer with my leg the way it was.

Very few turn roads veer off Coastal Highway to higher ground. When I thought of the tsunami swallowing my car, I glanced at the dashboard clock. The NOAA buoys that detected tsunamis were fairly accurate. Landfall would be between 7:40 and 7:55 p.m. The inland route might add ten minutes, but I'd still have enough time to warn the campers and guide them to the safety of the surrounding hillsides.

The fork in the road was upon me. To the left, the safer, longer route arced through the mountain pass. To the right, the more direct and dangerous highway followed the shoreline. My heart rate increased as I considered the real possibility of dying on Coastal Highway. Abruptly, I chose the mountain pass on Route 394, accelerated up the hills, and headed south through the dense forest away from the beach. I'd make it.

About five miles into my drive, I hit the traffic jam. People evacuating the seaside towns clogged the road, creating a crawling back-up. I banged my palm against the steering wheel over and over again until my hand ached. The perspiration on my neck and back had chilled, making my skin shiver as my pulse throbbed in my ears. The glowing numbers on my dashboard clock read 7:19 p.m. I had no time for this. Somehow, I hadn't thought about the evacuation. A long row of red brake lights disappeared around the mountain curve ahead of me.

I cursed myself for not taking Coastal Highway.

Plucking my cellphone out of my windbreaker, I started to dial Debbie back at the fire station. Maybe someone else at Company 3 was now free to go to Cedar Cliff, but I didn't know how to explain being in a traffic jam on Route 394 up in the hills. I pressed the "end call" button before the line started to ring.

Turning around to go back to Coastal Highway wouldn't work. I had gone too far already. Each moment ticked away on the glowing yellow lights of the dashboard clock. I applied the brakes repeatedly as the traffic crept slowly along the highway. In less than twenty minutes, the deadly wave would crash onto the shore. My mouth grew parched. A dull headache pressed hard against the back of my eyes. I had to think of something.

The traffic started to flow. We were moving again. Then I spotted a gravel shoulder beside the right-hand lane where the road widened in a valley ahead. I pressed the accelerator pedal to the floor until my engine roared, drove on the shoulder, and passed the cars and vans blocking my way.

I turned down the access road and sped past the wooden placard for Cedar Cliff Campground. My tires slid to a halt on the crushed stone of the upper parking lot. The campground was unusually quiet and still, with no campers anywhere in sight. The cabins appeared empty. A few unattended campfires crackled and glowed, thin bluish-gray smoke rising among the high branches of the redwoods and ponderosa pines. The campsites appeared completely normal, except all the people were gone. Maybe they had already abandoned this place and moved to higher ground, but both parking lots were full of cars and recreational vehicles. I climbed out of my Jeep. The woods were quiet, almost too quiet. No birds whistled or sang. No crickets chirped.

"Hey!" I yelled. "There's a tsunami! We gotta get out of here!"

No one replied. Only the crunching sounds of my footsteps on the loose stone parking lot broke the silence of the shadowy forest. My watch read 7:43 p.m.

"Hey!" I shouted again. "Anybody here? Hey!"

No one answered. They had to be around somewhere. I knew where I had to go. Leaving the safety of the upper parking lot, I descended the leaf-covered path toward the campsites near the beach. I hobbled to where the tree line ended. A wide passage between the gray and beige cliffs provided access to the shore.

I called out to evacuate the area. A young man and woman burst through the screen door of a wooden cabin, their faces panicked as they headed up the path to higher ground. I continued down the log stairs. No one else seemed to be in the cabins that lined the squat, grassy dunes beneath the cliffs.

My gut sank when I first saw the tsunami on the horizon. It appeared like the enormous ridgeline of a mountain range, dark and greenish-gray with sparse seafoam curling at its peak, silently accelerating toward the shore. I had only moments until I had to run back up the hillside, but there was just one cabin left.

"Tsunami! Hey, anybody in here?"

Farther away, blue and orange tents surrounded fire pits. Flapping towels and bathing suits hung on clotheslines. I had to escape now, if there was still time. I was fairly sure that no one was there, so I lumbered back up the hillside, my bad leg slowing me during my ascent up the slippery, leaf-covered path.

Something made me turn around. I had to see the wave. From halfway up the path amidst the trees, I had a better vantage of the unusually wide beach, which seemed three times its normal size. Shapes moved in the distance: the silhouettes of about a dozen people where the breakers reached the sand. I guessed they were curious why the beach had grown so large. They must not have known that the surf receded as an approaching tsunami gathered energy.

With all my strength, I screamed, "Hey! Over here! Hey! Tsunami! Behind you. Run!"

A few campers looked in my direction, but did not move. Then they turned toward the ocean as the shadow of the huge wall of water enshrouded them. They sprinted toward the camp; with all others soon following in a frenzied dash across the wide stretch of sand, but the wave was too fast.

I froze. My stomach tightened. The ocean swallowed them. I had failed.

The thunderous roar of water crashing onto the shore filled my ears, nearly knocking me over like cannon blasts from every direction. The flooding wave covered the sand, smashing the log cabins into splinters, ripping trees out of the soil with sickening crunches, and finally slamming into the surrounding cliffs. The steep rocks funneled the water toward me. I was still too close. A cold sheet of white spray fell over me. I grabbed the nearest tree trunk and locked my arms. The water rapidly churned up the hill, submerging me in the frigid flood that swirled and yanked me in its violent currents. I held my breath with my eyes sealed shut while the bark of the tree scraped against my forearms. Then the deluge began to recede back down the hill, pulling me hard toward the ocean. I held my grip. My lungs ached. I had been at the edge of the high water mark, but made it. I stood up, drenched in salt water, in shock, and not even sure if I was really still alive.

Channels of water around me ran down the mountain like instant streams. Waterfalls that had not been there moments before poured from the dark crags of the cliffs. Where a campground and a sandy beach once stood, now only a huge mass of ocean swirled, almost as if the sea was victorious in some ancient, mythical struggle between water and land. I scanned the surface for survivors, but there was no point. The campers who walked out onto the beach must have all died.

I couldn't control my rapid breathing. Wiping the dripping water off my face, I felt dizzy. As my knees started to buckle, I leaned against the tree that had kept the tsunami from sweeping me into the sea.

All those campers were gone. If I had taken Coastal Highway instead of Route 394, I would have arrived earlier and saved them.

The dark floodwaters between the cliffs rolled and tossed in the reddish glow of the sunset.

***

Twenty-four hours after the tsunami hit, the Coast Guard announced the end of the search and rescue mission. Now it was just recovery. None of us really expected to find any bodies, but we were wrong.

The next morning, members of our emergency teams and some civilian volunteers met at Fire Company 3 to walk the beaches south of Cedar Cliff Campground. I drove down Main Street where utility workers in a cherry picker were restringing powerlines. Locals with rakes and wheelbarrows removed broken branches from their front yards. Debbie Ortega was already outside Company 3 when I arrived on the back parking lot. She approached me with a surprised look across her face that somehow seemed motherly, which really wasn't what I wanted to see, so I brushed it off.

She reached out and gently touched my forearm. "You sure you're up for this, Peter?"

"Yeah," I replied. "I guess so."

"You don't have to."

"I know … but, um, it's okay. Besides, everyone else is going."

"I'll walk with you."

No one knew exactly where the currents would have taken the bodies after the massive tsunami waters withdrew back into the Pacific Ocean. The currents generally moved in a southerly direction along the coastline, so that's where we would begin today. The fire chief tapped his index finger on the large county map just inside the overhead doors and assigned each of us a two-mile stretch of beach. I offered to drive to our assigned location, but Debbie insisted we take her rusty minivan.

The sun warmed the morning air. A soft, salty breeze blew the dune grasses to and fro. We crossed the beach until we reached the darker sands that showed the high-tide mark of last night. It would've been a nice day for a stroll on the beach, if we weren't looking for the remains of the victims.

Small, gentle waves glided from the calm ocean toward us. The distant horizon was flat, unlike two days ago. My eyes kept returning to the horizon as we started our search. In my mind, I could still see the huge wall of water heading toward me and slamming on top of the campers as they sprinted across the beach.

"I know you can't go real fast," Debbie said, not mentioning my prosthetic leg expressly. "We'll take our time."

"Thanks. You don't sink in the sand as much where it's dry."

For twenty minutes or so, we walked together in silence. Usually, the shoreline gradually sloped from the hillsides to the breakers, but the tsunami had piled the sands into oddly-shaped dunes and canyons. Other than the torn-up beach, we saw nothing unusual as we worked our way south.

Debbie asked, "I suppose that maybe I shouldn't ask you this, but how'd you do at the Coroner's Inquiry?"

"Fine, I guess. It was just the preliminary."

"I've never been to one. Is it okay if I …?"

"Sure," I replied, not wanting her to dance around the subject. "To be honest with you, the inquiry was fairly informal. Just an interview, really. A couple, maybe in their twenties, went first. I saw them at the campground just before the tsunami made landfall. They testified about how many campers were staying in their area, but they weren't really sure. They heard me calling for the evacuation and sprinted up the mountain. That was about it."

"And you went next?"

"Right. I told the panel how I went to Cedar Cliff because I thought they might not know about the tsunami. I described how I went through the cabins looking for people, what I saw, and how about a dozen people had walked far out on the beach just before it hit. I yelled out to them, but … well … not in enough time."

"Look, we all know how it turned out, but if you really think about it, you're a hero in all this."

I didn't feel that way, so I said nothing. Maybe now I could tell her why I had arrived late at the campground. The coroner didn't ask me about that, and I didn't volunteer anything. I would have told him the truth, if he had asked. Maybe now I could be honest. If anyone would understand why I took Route 394 instead of Coastal Highway, it would be Debbie. I just hadn't thought about a traffic jam during the evacuation, but I should have. I shouldn't have taken the safer route, but when it came down to it, I failed everyone. Maybe Debbie would understand, but then again, maybe not. I held it all in and continued walking. Tiny sandpipers stabbed their beaks into the damp sand and scurried off as we grew closer.

The distant horizon over the ocean still appeared level and serene.

A small mass rested ahead of us where the waves lapped ashore. Debbie ran ahead of me. I followed her as quickly as I could. She arrived first and knelt down. She turned toward me, held up her hand, and said, "Stay back."

I ignored her and came closer until I saw the body of the little girl, maybe ten or eleven years old, lying in the surf. Her hair drifted back and forth in the undulating waves. Debbie felt for a carotid pulse, but did not start CPR or any resuscitation. She slowly withdrew her fingers from the sides of the little girl's neck, turned to me teary-eyed, and shook her head. I couldn't take my eyes off the child's face, which appeared so peaceful, almost like she was sleeping, but she was dead.

Debbie contacted Company 3 for medical transport and told me to wait on Coastal Highway to flag down the paramedics. When I reached the asphalt shoulder, I broke down, unable to hold it together any longer. At least up on the road, Debbie wouldn't see me like this. I composed myself before anyone arrived. The paramedics slid the stretcher covered with a small white sheet into the back of the ambulance and drove toward Ambrose without turning on their lights or siren.

From that moment on, I wasn't able to shake the memory of that little girl's face.

A red and white Coast Guard helicopter zigzagged along the coast in a search pattern near us, but nothing ever came of it. Debbie said she would continue along the beach on her own, but that wasn't fair to her. I walked a few steps behind her, not intending to get close to any other bodies. We didn't find any. None of the other search teams on the beach or the Coast Guard patrols over the water located any victims.

By the end of the day, the sheriff had identified how many people stayed at Cedar Cliff two nights ago. The surviving campers were accounted for, but a total of thirteen people were still missing and presumed drowned. The little girl on the beach was the only body ever recovered. The ocean had claimed the rest forever.

For hours that night, I could not sleep. When I finally did drift off, I didn't get any real rest. Nightmares came in rapid succession. Images of the huge wave crashing down on the campers as they ran across the beach kept jarring me awake. Floodwaters engulfed me as I held tightly to the tree trunk, the violent currents pulling me toward the deep sea. That little girl's gray face stared lifelessly up at the morning sky, turned to me, and whispered, "Why?"

More than anything else over the next week, the face of that drowned little girl haunted me. I saw her unblinking eyes in dark computer screens, store windows, and even the deep shadows of the long stairwell to my apartment. I wasn't superstitious at all. I knew that my imagination was running amok. Still, I couldn't control those visions. The whole ordeal had shattered my psyche. Maybe I was actually going crazy, seeing things that couldn't be there. I requested temporary leave from my job at Company 3. Someone else could take over my shift at the Communications Center for a while. When the nightmares got worse over the next few weeks, I quit altogether. My supervisor pleaded with me to stay, but there was no way I could do my job anymore.

Debbie Ortega drove to my apartment and begged me to speak with a counselor, explaining there was no shame in needing a little help once in a while, but that wouldn't be for me. Besides, she didn't know the full story, and I couldn't tell her now. Not ever. Not to anyone. All those campers drowned in the tsunami because I was afraid. Somehow I had to find a way to go on living, knowing what kind of person I really was.

***

For a year, I was adrift. I floated between dead-end jobs, spent days in bed until noon or so, and sat for long evenings in dive bars far from Ambrose. Too many people knew me in town. Kentucky bourbon became my favorite with its smooth first sip and fiery afterburn. A few of those, man, and you felt all right. Even this world can start to seem all right, if just for a short while. At first, I sampled the premium brands, but eventually worked my way down to the lower shelves at Victory Liquor Store. When I had nearly depleted my savings account, I was throwing back shots from plastic gallon jugs with labels that claimed to contain real bourbon, but I wasn't so sure. I doubt there was ever a bearded preacher named Ezekiel Calhoun with a distillery on Mulberry Creek, but the brand history on the back label was amusing. I wasn't going for taste, just the volume that allowed me to sleep without dreaming. Most nights I had Ezekiel to thank for that.

Not everyone would've reacted the way I did. I knew that. I didn't like where I was heading, but every time I decided to give up the booze, a few nights later I would find myself drifting back into some dark bar. The conversations with whoever sat next to me were always pointless, though usually pleasant. The televisions sets on the walls showed endless baseball games that no one watched, except me. At least I was getting out of my apartment now and again.

One night after the last call at Slacky Jack's Tavern, I got behind the wheel of my Jeep when I was way over the limit. An Oregon state trooper passed me in the other direction when I weaved a bit over the double yellow line. I watched him in my rear view mirror as he turned around and flipped on his red and blues. Figuring that I probably had this coming, I pulled onto the shoulder. He parked his squad car behind me and stopped. Then he sped down the highway. He must have received a more important call than a routine DWI investigation, so he left me on the side of the road. After a few minutes, I drove home as carefully as possible. When I dragged my blankets up and collapsed into my pillow, I realized that the state trooper probably got a call from the Communications Center in my old fire station, but I didn't think about that until I was ready to pass out.

Local bartenders had started connecting patrons with designated drivers on a phone app called "D-Sig-N8." I'd heard about it, but never used it. I debated quitting drinking for good, and even stopped for a while, but then the nightmares started up again. I'd wake up after seeing the tsunami, the flooding waters covering me, and the girl on the beach with her dead green eyes staring upwards as the foamy surf flowed back and forth over her face. After a week without bourbon, I caught glimpses of her lifeless eyes while I was awake, staring at me from dark corners and in glass reflections.

I wasn't losing my mind, because they were just dreams, and minor hallucinations were just a trick of my imagination. If you knew these things weren't real, then you couldn't be crazy. There was no way I was going to sit back on some quack psychiatrist's sofa, explain ink blots to him, talk about my feelings, and then swallow a fistful of pills. I just needed some more time on my own, that was all.

Soon I was asking bartenders to text drivers for me on the D-Sig-N8 app whenever I'd had my fill of Kentucky bourbon. The driver service was simple and cheap, certainly less expensive than the fines, attorney fees, and other costs of a DWI. I liked using the app so much that I considered becoming a driver, especially when my ATM card didn't work one afternoon and I realized I was flat broke. My rent was due in a week and I'd be short, so I signed up. I picked the late schedules on Thursdays, Fridays, and Saturdays when the bars were crowded. I vowed to stay sober those nights, at least until I got back to my apartment after my shift.

Saturday was the first day of the college football season. Fans would pack the sports bars. I could pocket a wallet full of green and maybe even afford a bottle of something that didn't smell like diluted wood varnish. Still, when I thought about it, I didn't want to be on the road that night, the one year anniversary of the tsunami. I could just hang at home, but the overdue bills on my kitchen table persuaded me to grab my keys and switch on my phone for ride requests. Sometimes it was just good to drive and clear my head.

I dropped off a few people here and there, nothing special. Around 10:15 p.m., my phone chimed. The ride request made little sense. The starting point was Cascade Trading Post, which must have closed hours ago. There was no definite destination, just a line stating "About twenty miles." The pick-up time was now.

I texted a quick reply asking for more details, mostly so I could negotiate the price. The evening was slow, so when I didn't get an immediate response, I wrote back $30.00. Starting high allowed me room to haggle. The reply text simply read "Great!" followed by one of those irksome smiley faces.

A young woman in a plaid shirt, khaki shorts, and hiking boots stood on the steps of Cascade Trading Post when I arrived. Moths and gnats swarmed the florescent porch light above her head. Her auburn hair was braided in long pigtails. She might have been in her mid-twenties, but who can tell these days? The young woman smiled shyly when I glided to a stop and then tossed her knapsack over her shoulder. I started to get out of my Jeep to help her load any other bags, but she popped open the backseat door and climbed inside.

"You got everything?" I asked, refastening my seatbelt.

"Yeah, thanks. Just some camping supplies," she replied.

"No bags?"

"All in here," she said, thumping her knapsack.

"Okay, then. Where're you headin' exactly?"

"I didn't know how to load it into D-Sig-N8, if that's how you say it. I did the best I could."

"Twenty miles or so didn't give me much to go on."

"Sorry about that. Down Coastal Highway. South of town. I'll recognize it when we get close."

"You sure? There's not much between Ambrose and the next town."

"Yeah, no prob."

I turned the key in the ignition. A loud commercial for discount mattresses blared over the speakers, so to be somewhat polite I asked what kind of music she liked. She said that she didn't mind the quiet. Taking the hint, I turned off the radio.

Before dropping the automatic transmission into drive, I said, "Thirty, okay? Cash only."

"Uh-huh. Just get me there before our campfire is out."

After passing the last streetlight in town, I headed south toward the intersection of Route 394 and Coastal Highway. Exactly one year ago I had taken the mountain pass and gotten bottled up in a traffic jam during the evacuation. If I had stayed on Coastal Highway, a lot of things would've been different right now. I pressed the accelerator and blew past the turn for Route 394.

The curves of the road followed the rocky shoreline with its patches of wide sand. To my left were the mountains, dark and towering. To my right, a bright crescent moon rose over the black ocean with its long waves cresting in white near the shore. The sea appeared strangely peaceful. My headlights illuminated the winding road. I kept my focus forward, unwilling to look toward the ocean for any length of time. Sure, I could still clearly remember the deadly wall of water that had crashed into the shore. All the details of that night were still fresh, like they were about to happen again, but I put them out of my mind. I was so much better than I was even just a few months ago. I was going to beat this, not let it hold me in its grasp forever. I kind of wished I had the radio on. My young passenger fidgeted with her knapsack and accidentally bumped the back of my seat.

I said, "We're almost at twenty miles. Give me some warning when we get close, all right?"

"I remember some signs."

"Mile markers?"

"Yeah, something like that," she replied.

Along a straight stretch of highway, I got my Jeep up to fifty miles per hour, figuring I'd have time for more runs back in town.

"So you're camping this weekend?" I asked.

"Yup. Me and my family. The woods are like really beautiful this time of year. Warm days. Cool nights. You know, totally awesome."

"Nice up here. I guess you're backwoods camping, huh?"

"No, some campground my folks like."

"Campground?" I asked. "There hasn't been a campground out here for a year."

She asked, "Am I dead?"

I glanced in the rear view mirror, but the backseat was empty. She was gone.

***

Every hair on the back of my neck stood on end. I pulled my Jeep onto the side of the road, not really sure what had just happened. All the car doors were locked. Maybe my overactive imagination had gotten the better of me. Maybe I was just worn down and needed sleep. Or maybe I had actually lost my mind. I activated the D-Sig-N8 app on my phone and saw the ride request from the woman at Cascade Trading Post just a half hour ago. No one walked along the empty road around me. The woods along the hillsides were absolutely still. I rolled down my window and listened. A distant owl screeched into the night, but otherwise the dark trees towered over me in silence.

Adrenaline surged through my bloodstream, so I took a few deep breaths and called Debbie Ortega back at Fire Company 3. Instead of the recorded landline at the Communications Center, I dialed her personal cellphone.

"Hi, Debbie," I said as calmly as possible.

"Peter? Is that you?"

"Uh-huh."

"Oh, wow. Great to hear from you. Hey, I thought about you this evening."

"Yeah, tonight's the one-year anniversary."

"You okay?" she asked, sounding genuinely concerned.

"Yeah, I suppose … well, no, not really." I looked up and down the road for a young woman with braided pigtails who wasn't there.

"What's wrong?" Debbie asked.

"Just tell me if anything unusual is going on tonight?"

"Well, there was a commemoration service for the tsunami victims in front of Town Hall this afternoon, but that wrapped up hours ago."

"No, not like that," I replied. "Anything strange."

"Strange? Like what?"

"I don't know. Weird 911 calls."

"No. It's pretty quiet. You don't sound so good. What's wrong?"

"Aw, nothing, I guess."

Neither of us spoke for a few seconds. No headlights from other cars illuminated the winding highway before me. The muffled, rhythmic sounds of the crashing waves echoed off the dark sea cliffs.

Debbie said, "You know, Peter, you can always talk to me."

"You don't know how much I appreciate that. I mean it."

"So, why'd you call?"

"I … I can't. You wouldn't believe me."

"Come on. Until you open up, you're just going to spiral. You should be back here at the fire station. It's just not the same without your ridiculous sticky notes all over the place. If not me, then someone else can get you past this. I think we can get your old job back. You need to be here taking 911 calls and helping people, okay?"

My cellphone chimed. I took the phone away from my ear. The screen displayed another ride request on the D-Sig-N8 app.

"Debbie, I got to go."

"Peter …"

"Not now. Maybe later."

She said nothing, but I somehow sensed her disappointment. I quietly said "Bye," as I broke off the connection and replied to the ride request. Some dude with the screen name "Mondo-Man" needed a lift from Palmero's Sports Grill to the Blue Sky Motel. When he agreed to pay a quick twelve-dollar fare, I was happy to head back toward the streetlights in town and pick him up.

Mondo-Man waited for me on the sidewalk outside Palmero's with a bored-looking middle-aged woman wearing too much make-up and a lumpy dress. If I had to guess from his appearance, gray-haired Mondo-Man was a former lineman for some college football team, and now he sold insurance between telling stories of his past glories on the field. He probably trolled the bars at night looking for potential clients or whatever else came along. I rarely shook hands with a rider, but after what just happened up the highway, I did in this case. Mondo-Man's hand was real – real fat and real sweaty.

Mondo-Man was courteous and attentive with the woman, and even opened the car door for her, which made me fairly certain she wasn't his wife. I dropped them off at the Blue Sky Motel. I don't think the woman spoke a word during the entire ride. Mondo-Man slid me a twenty and said, "No change, bud." He gave me a knowing look that I took to mean he'd call me in a few hours for a ride back to town. I thanked him and thought about some local bars where I could toss back a shot or two, even though I knew I shouldn't. I checked my cellphone. A ride request was waiting unanswered on the D-Sig-N8 app. My phone hadn't chimed, which was weird. Maybe I had accidentally hit the mute button.

Someone all the way down in Culbert wanted a ride back here to Ambrose, a fifty-mile round trip along Coastal Highway that would take me past Cedar Cliff Campground, or at least where it had been before the tsunami. I didn't really want to drive that far, so I texted a quote of one hundred dollars, figuring that would get rid of him.

The reply text said, "Deal."

Somebody had to be pretty desperate for a ride, but with all those overdue bills on my kitchen table, I resigned myself to take the job. Besides, I couldn't keep avoiding the memories of the tsunami forever. I had to beat this. If I drove past the abandoned campground, maybe I could somehow prove to myself that I could cope with reminders of the disaster. Maybe taking that drive would finally get me past the nightmares and the sudden, uncontrollable visions.

I figured a guy with the name Mondo-Man would be at least a couple hours at the motel, so I confirmed the ride request and headed south for the pick-up.

My Jeep was a mile or so from Cedar Cliff when a pungent odor wafted through the vents, a thick smell similar to a wet campfire. I fiddled with the vents and scanned my dashboard for mechanical problems, but nothing appeared to be wrong. The stench of damp ashes grew stronger, so I opened the windows. The smoky smell was not outside and soon dissipated as I drove down the highway. I rolled the windows back up, figuring that I'd probably have to call my mechanic tomorrow.

Then I sensed someone breathing heavily close to the back of my neck. Behind me, a low, growling voice said, "You've trapped us. Release us."

Startled, I looked in my rear-view mirror. A transparent rotting corpse sat in the back of my Jeep. Seaweed, barnacles, and writhing worms encrusted its ghostly skull. Blood red eyes glared at me as the corpse leaned forward and grabbed my shoulders with wet, bony hands.

Panicked, I slammed on the brakes. My tires screeched. The Jeep clipped the guardrail at the edge of a steep overhang and lurched like it was about to flip over, but somehow stayed upright. The car spun sideways on the roadway before coming to a stop above the beach and the churning ocean waves. Everything seemed to happen in slow motion. When I gathered my bearings, my headlights shone on the distant, rocky crags of Cedar Cliff.

Then my car engine shut off on its own, and the electrical system died. In total darkness, I struggled to unfasten my seatbelt and jump out of the car while the growling corpse shifted around in the back seat.

"Yes, let's go," the transparent corpse sneered, encouraging me to exit my Jeep. "Come with me ... into the water."

"No," I screamed. "Get out of here!"

"Then I'll wait for you, follow you everywhere. You hold us in the dark waters, Peter. Let us go."

"Hold you?" I asked, my heart pounding in my chest, too afraid to move. At least the ghostly corpse was not reaching for me.

"We can't leave without you. You were meant to be in the ocean with us, but you resisted the pull of the wave. Come, join us in the sea."

"No! I'm not going."

"You must," the ghost growled. "You've trapped us in these waters. Do what's right. We shall walk into the dark waters together."

"No, you're wrong. I don't trap you. How could I trap you?"

"You know, Peter. You know."

"Because I arrived too late to warn you about the tsunami? Because I didn't get swept away with you? I tried to warn you."

"No. Not what you did back then. You hold us now."

"Look, it was a mistake. A terrible mistake. I've had to live with that for the past year. But I didn't mean for you to die, for anyone to die. I went to the campground to save you. I was just ..."

The ghost leaned toward me and whispered, "There's nothing to be afraid of, Peter."

"I'm sorry. Really, I am. Look, my leg is bad. Always has been. I can't swim. Nobody can change what happened last year at the campground."

"No, you can't."

"I was just ..." I swallowed hard. "I was scared. Is that what you need me to admit? Okay, then. I'll say it. I'm a coward. I was afraid of the tsunami, so

I took the long way to the Cedar Cliff Campground. You died because of me. There's nothing I can do now."

"Yes there is, Peter. Release us. Let us go."

"I'm not holding you."

"Come, walk into the dark water," the ghost said in a voice like a hissing lizard. "It's better if you choose to join us. End this for us. End it for you. Come now to the sea, or we must come for you." The ghost's words faded away into the darkness. A faint odor of damp firewood lingered in the air. I was alone again.

I turned the key in the ignition, but my Jeep wouldn't start. I tried again with no result and slammed my palm against the steering wheel. The battery seemed to be drained. Even the interior lights didn't switch on when I twisted the key. I grabbed my cellphone to call for help, but there was no reception out here by Cedar Cliff. My call attempt failed. Out in the roiling ocean, I saw pale-blue spots shimmer just beneath the breakers.

A tiny voice, perhaps that of a little girl, broke the silence. "Mister, don't let them take you." No one else was inside my car. The roadway around me was deserted. The soft voice seemed to come out of nowhere, yet was all around me.

"Who's that?" I asked.

"Molly," the disembodied voice replied sheepishly. "I'm really not supposed to talk to strangers."

"It's okay, Molly. Where are you?"

"Right here. But I won't let you see me, 'cause I'm so ..." Her voice trailed off.

In my rear-view mirror, I saw only two small eyes. They were the eyes of the little girl that Debbie and I found dead on the beach, the same eyes that had haunted me over the past year in dim shadows and reflections. The back seat was empty.

"It's all right, Molly," I replied.

"They're coming for you now."

Glowing transparent corpses crept through the cresting waves onto the sand. About a dozen ghosts slowly crawled on all fours toward my disabled

Jeep. Some were skeletal; others were bloated, decaying bodies. One by one, they stood up and headed in my direction with their bony arms reaching outward. Their dark, lifeless eyes focused directly at me.

"What can I do, Molly? The tsunami scared me. I chickened out when you needed me. I'm sorry you died. Sorry to all of you."

"You just don't get it, do you, Mister? It's not saying that you're sorry. You have to forgive yourself."

"I don't understand."

The little girl replied, "I didn't know how to tell you – but it's you. We're stuck here because of what you're thinking – and, um, feeling. Your memories and stuff. Don't feel so guilty. It's okay. Let go. Let us go."

"You know what I did, Molly."

"Yup, and it's all right. Now there're only two ways. The others see only one, but there're two. Forgive yourself … or come into the ocean with us."

"How can I forgive myself?"

Her eyes faded and disappeared in the rear-view mirror before she answered me. Molly was gone.

The glowing, bluish-white ghosts slowly crawled across the beach toward me, weaving around the jagged rocks, growing closer to the dunes at the edge of the road. I still couldn't start my car. There was nowhere to run. The ghost closest to me approached the guardrail next to my disabled Jeep.

From all around me, the snarling voices of the ghosts echoed, "Peter, it's time. Come to the water … come into the water."

Guilt had ruined my life. The deaths of these campers had been my fault, because I had been afraid. Yes, I was a coward. My fear cost these people their lives. Now my shame and guilt trapped them in the dark waters where they died. I had to fix this and release them. I'd confess to Debbie Ortega why the campers drowned, even if she lost all respect for me and ended our friendship forever. I'd tell her the truth. Maybe she'd understand, and if she didn't, then at least I'd be honest with her – and myself. I'd go back to work at the Communications Center at the fire station again, if the chief would let me. If not, then I'd find a job helping people elsewhere. And I'd never touch booze again. I'd even see a counselor.

It was time to let go of my mistake and move forward again.

I gripped the steering wheel, closed my eyes, and whispered into the darkness, "I forgive myself."

I opened my eyes. The ghosts creeping toward me rose above the beach and dissolved into glowing clouds of pale blue mist. The shapeless clouds floated away from me, glided over the ocean, and disappeared at the horizon. They were free. I was free.

I turned the ignition key, and to my surprise, the engine restarted. I could have taken the mountain road home, but instead I drove back to Ambrose along Coastal Highway. I rolled down my window to take in the cool ocean breeze. Light from the crescent moon sparkled atop the curling waves that landed gently along the shore.

Aunt Olga and the Werewolf
KM Rockwood

Aunt Olga sat on a roughhewn bench outside her cottage door. Despite the warm morning sunlight, she had her shawl drawn tightly around her shoulders. Her wrinkled chin rested on her hands, which in turn rested on the handle of her knurled walking stick.

Sandor stopped his cart by the front gate, tying the pony to a post.

The two ever-curious goats stuck their heads through the woven fence, their dark eyes intent on the pony and their jaws chewing nonstop.

"Let me come and help you get up, Auntie," Sandor shouted as he opened the gate.

"Nonsense," Aunt Olga replied, grasping her stick and heaving herself to her feet. "I may have a touch of arthritis, but I don't need help to walk."

More than a "touch," Sandor thought as he watched her weave her way down the path to the gate. Every time it was his turn to pick her up for church on Sunday morning, she was frailer than the last.

His cousin, Zoltan, whose turn it was to bring her last week, had warned him. "I was late already, and then I had to go home for my cart. She could barely make it down the path, much less all the way to church. By the time we arrived at church, the service was halfway over, and she was angry."

Sandor shook his head. "But what can we expect? She was old when I was a child. Does anybody know how old she really is?"

Aunt Olga was the last of her generation. Sandor, Zoltan and four other cousins took turns picking her up for church and then bringing her to their homes to share Sunday dinner. They knew that, at least once a week, she got a good meal, cooked by their sturdy wives, who then packed leftovers and garden produce for her to take home. For several years now, the garden plot next to her cottage had lain fallow. Sandor thought perhaps that food they supplied and the goat milk might be all she had to eat.

When Aunt Olga reached the gate, Sandor picked her up and swung her into the cart. She looked scrawny, but he was surprised at how stiff and heavy she felt.

"I can climb in myself, thank you," Aunt Olga huffed, but it was too late. She settled herself on a pile of hay he had in the back of the cart. When he dropped her off, he would pitch the hay into the shed for the goats.

He clucked to his pony, and they started toward town, Sandor walking beside the cart.

"Auntie," he said. "Do you think perhaps it's time for you to move closer to town? You're so isolated in that house, and you're not getting any younger. Perhaps you should move in with one of us."

"Nonsense," was Olga's reply.

Sandor was relieved to hear that. His wife would not be happy with the idea of Aunt Olga moving into their tiny house—they were crowded already, with another baby due in the fall—nor would the wives of any of the cousins be happy with the idea. But she was not safe alone way out here, especially not with the rumors of werewolves once again roaming the hills.

Sandor and his cousins, as well as their wives, knew their obligations to family, and all of them had taken a sacred oath to their fathers that they would not abandon Aunt Olga in her old age. As far as Sandor knew, she was an only child of aging parents, and had lived in the cottage her entire life. She had cared for her elderly parents until their deaths, and continued to live in the cottage alone. Leaving it for a house nearer to town and crowded with children would be difficult for everyone.

Aunt Olga had never married, never had a suitor, and so she had no children of her own to look after her.

Sandor dreaded the day one of them would come up to the cottage and Aunt Olga would not be sitting on the bench. He hoped he would not be the one who had to enter the dark, musty interior to find her lying in her bed, having died in her sleep. Uneasily, he considered the much more distressing possibility that she might fall ill or be injured, and lie there for days unable to help herself.

Ashamed at feeling so relieved that Aunt Olga wouldn't be moving in with *his* family, he tried a new tactic. "At least, Auntie, let me take your goats. I will make sure they are well cared for. And I will send one of the children to deliver the milk every day." And to check up on her.

"Nonsense." That seemed to be Aunt Olga's favorite new word. "I take perfectly good care of my goats. I milk them three times a day, which is more than you would be able to do. And sometimes I make goat cheese, which I can sell at the market. Everybody knows my goat cheese is good! The best."

In years past, Aunt Olga had cared for a much larger herd of goats. Sandor could not remember her bringing cheese to the market in over a decade. Or even making it to the market herself. Perhaps he had been remiss not to offer to take her some time? He said, "Your goat cheese is wonderful. The best anyone has ever tasted. But we do worry about you, alone out here, with no one to protect you."

"Worry about me? What is there to worry about?"

Sandor almost said, "Besides you falling ill or hurting yourself, and no one coming around for days to check up on you?" But she would not want to hear that.

Instead, he said, "You know, Auntie, there have been reports of werewolves in the hills."

"Werewolves! Now, when I was a young girl, werewolves did roam the hills. But there have been none in years. Every time a sheep wanders away or a calf is lost, someone starts a rumor that the werewolves are back. And yet no one ever sees one."

"Johan, the shepherd, said he saw a werewolf at the last full moon. Three weeks ago. It took one of his lambs. He had his slingshot, and he was sure he hit it right in the haunches with a big stone. It got away with the lamb, but it was limping badly. And it left some drops of blood."

Aunt Olga snorted. "More likely a big dog that some irresponsible town person let out to run at night."

"We worry about you, Aunt Olga. If there is a werewolf, it might come down out of the hills, looking for food. Especially if Johan did wound it and it's injured. Your cottage and your goat shed are right here, where it would pass by to get to any of the other farms. It's not safe."

"I would think that if one of your werewolves were going to bother me, it would have done so long ago. Nothing has changed over the years."

Sandor persisted. "Auntie, you have only a run-in shed for the goats. I know it keeps them out of the weather and it's snug enough, even in winter, but a werewolf could easily get in."

"I am in no more danger from werewolves than I have ever been. Nor are my goats."

"Or if someone were letting a large dog roam …"

"People should not keep dogs they can't handle."

"That may be, but it won't help if one gets into your goat shed."

"So what do you propose to do?"

Sandor reached over and patted the pony's rump. At night, he locked his animals in a snug, secure barn. "Auntie, you can go in your cottage and bar the door, so you would be safe. But the goats won't be safe in that shed. Maybe let me take the goats for a few days and lock them in our barn at night. At least until the full moon is past."

"No, thank you." Aunt Olga pulled her shawl tighter around her shoulders, her mouth set in a firm line. "It's not that I don't appreciate you trying to help. But I can take care of myself. And my goats."

If her goats were attacked, Sandor had no doubt that Aunt Olga would try to save them. She could do no good for the goats, and she would be putting herself in danger.

As if she were reading his thoughts, Aunt Olga said, "Werewolves fear fire. If one came around, I would make a torch and chase it off. That's what people used to do when I was young. Everything will be fine."

Sandor doubted that.

After church, he gathered Zoltan, Gregor, and the other cousins. They agreed that Aunt Olga's goats made a tempting target for a crippled werewolf. And, if it attacked, she would come to their aid. She might light a torch, but if she did, she would be fortunate not to set the shed or the cottage on fire.

"We must go stand guard," Sandor said with a sigh.

"All of us?" Gregor asked. "We have our own homesteads to guard."

"Maybe just two of us at a time?"

"If she doesn't want our help, why should we put ourselves out?" Zoltan complained.

"Because." Sandor's piercing gaze moved from one cousin to the next. "It is our duty. And we have all promised our fathers to care for Aunt Olga in her old age."

"Why don't we just insist she move closer to town?" Gregor asked.

"She doesn't want to," Sandor reminded him. "And where would she go? Would your wife be happy if she moved in with you?"

Gregor looked at the ground. "No."

"We only need to do it the night of the full moon, which is this Friday," Sandor said. "Zoltan and I will take this one. We can build a small fire and make some torches out of twisted straw."

"Straw torches against a werewolf?"

"They fear fire. And then, in a few months, if there are no more sightings, we can rethink it. Perhaps the werewolf will move on."

"Or die," Gregor said.

"Or die," Sandor agreed.

The next Friday evening, Sandor made sure his wife and children were secure in the house, and the livestock in the barn. "No matter what," he warned them, "don't go outside. Bar the door. Don't open it for anything or anyone but me. And before you do open the door, make very sure it is me."

For those standing watch, fire would be their first defense, but Sandor wanted backup. He tucked his wife's butchering knife at his waist and looked among his tools, selecting a pitchfork and a scythe. Not ideal weapons, but they would have to do.

Zoltan, as usual, was late, and by the time they headed up the twisting road toward Aunt Olga's cottage, the moon was already rising.

A howl filled the air.

They looked uneasily at each other. Zoltan hefted the club he carried. "I wish we were archers," he said. "I would much rather stand back and put an arrow through a werewolf than try to chase it off with a torch. Or fight it at close quarters."

Sweat beading on his forehead, Sandor broke into a swift trot, his hobnailed boots raising plumes of dust which trailed behind him. Holding the long-handled tools was awkward, and he almost tripped. Regaining his footing, he tossed the scythe aside, and clutched the pitchfork in one hand. With his other hand, he held the handle of the knife at his belt and resumed running.

Zoltan's heavy footsteps and heavier breathing fell farther and farther behind him.

The bleat of a frightened goat reached his ears.

Pushing himself to run faster, Sandor rounded the last twist in the road.

In the dimming twilight, he could see the goats rush from one side of the enclosure to the other, throwing themselves against the fence, their ears twitching madly and their nostrils flared in terror.

In the center of the pen, a dark, furred creature crouched on all fours, its gaze following the goats as they stampeded in panic. As Sandor approached, the creature turned its head to look at him.

Beneath its pointed ears, beady yellow eyes glowered at him. It lifted its massive snout to sniff the air. Saliva dripped from its sharp fangs. Was this what a werewolf looked like? Could it possibly be a huge dog turned out to run at night, like Aunt Olga thought?

Sandor glanced toward the cottage. The door stood open. Aunt Olga must have heard the commotion the goats made, and come out to see what was disturbing them.

But where was she? Sandor scanned the area. The light was failing, and he couldn't see her anywhere in the shadows. Nor did he see a limp form that could have been her frail body.

Perhaps she had dashed back into the cottage to light a torch. Sandor hoped she had, and that she would come rushing out with it now.

The creature, werewolf or dog, turned it fiery eyes toward him. They were the eyes of an evil creature, a crazed creature, but an intelligent creature.

A werewolf.

Keeping the fence between himself and the werewolf, Sandor raised his pitchfork. The snarling werewolf gathered its feet underneath it, ready to spring. He could smell its hot breath.

The pitchfork, which he had thought would make a reasonable weapon when he'd seized it, now seemed flimsy and inadequate. But it was all he had. He braced its handle against his chest and held the tines steady, pointing up and out.

As it launched itself at him, Sandor shifted the pitchfork so it met the werewolf at the height of its leap.

The handle of the pitchfork drove into Sandor's chest, knocking him over backwards. With a loud snap, the handle broke. His head hit the ground hard. The shattered piece from the pitchfork fell from his hand and rolled away.

Sandor's chest felt on fire, and the thought that he might never be able to breathe again flitted through his mind. The back of his head ached and every bone in his body felt like it had shattered.

But he had to get up. He couldn't lie there and let the werewolf attack. And what of Aunt Olga?

He scrambled up, shaking his head to clear his vision. Every second he expected to smell the foul breath of the werewolf on his face and feel its savage teeth tear into his flesh.

But when he regained his feet and looked, he saw that the werewolf had turned away from him. It was crawling toward the cottage door, barely able to pull itself along. It left a bloody trail in its wake.

Sandor tried to shout to Aunt Olga to shut the door, to hide, to climb up on a piece of furniture, but he couldn't catch his breath and the warning stuck in his throat.

He pulled the knife from his waistband and forced his trembling hand to grasp it.

Staggering forward, he followed the werewolf to the doorstep, where it paused and turned to face him.

The pitchfork was embedded deep in its chest. Blood gushed from its mouth and nose. It snarled and tried to gather its feet under itself, but instead it swayed and collapsed, its eyes never leaving Sandor's face. But the fiery glow was growing dim.

The snarl turned into a cough. The creature's limbs trembled and its body writhed in agony.

As he watched, the werewolf began to change shape. The long nose shortened, the sharp teeth shrank into its mouth, the pointed ears disappeared, the fur dissolved to expose naked pink flesh, the limbs grew longer and more slender.

Zoltan, his breathe coming in gasps, came up behind Sandor. "What is it?"

Sandor chest hurt and he struggled to say anything. But even if he could talk, he could not have found any words to describe what he was seeing.

"Why, it's Aunt Olga!" Zoltan cried, clutching his club. "She's having some kind of seizure. And where are her clothes? I thought it was a werewolf!"

Sandor stared in fascinated horror as the writhing grew feebler and the creature lay still.

He managed to gasp out, "It was."

The Incident at Deep Lake

BG House

Albert Salinger rowed the rented boat through the wisps of fog coming off the surface of Deep Lake. No deadlines for a whole weekend. The exhausted professor planned to birdwatch, row out on the lake, and relax for a few days after the midterms. The boat creaked as he dipped the oars into the water. He hadn't rowed a boat in ages. He could still handle a boat at a good clip, but the ache in his muscles proved he was out of shape.

Red sky in morning, sailor's warning. The crimson dawn sky above the hills brought the ominous old weather saying to mind.

He caught his breath. Thick bubbles rose to the surface of the lake a mere thirty feet away. Baffled, he stopped rowing to gape at the water. He was in the Virginia Blue Ridge Mountains, not Florida, so an alligator couldn't be lurking under the surface.

The eerie call of a loon echoed against the tree line.

A sharp sound blasted through the woods. Seconds later, Albert jerked backward. He grabbed his left shoulder as pain ripped through his body. It took a moment for him to realize what happened. *Shot, damn it.* He brought his hand down from his wounded shoulder, watched his palm drip with blood, and passed out.

After a while, he regained hazy consciousness. The rowboat's bow had grounded on the stony bank while the stern drifted back and forth in the water. With what strength he had left, he crawled out onto the rocky shore and managed to stagger three paces before he collapsed.

His phone rang in his jacket, but he couldn't reach it.

Someone fired more shots. This time they flew over his head.

Hoping the shooter couldn't see him, he lay motionless even though searing pain ran through his shoulder. Blood soaked his clothes. His limbs began to grow cold. He was probably going into shock.

Branches and twigs broke around him. He caught sight of a coonhound barreling toward him and felt the dog sniff at his crotch.

Get that damn dog off me, for God's sake.

The shooter had to be nearby. The ground trembled. He heard footsteps. Closing his eyes, he intended to play dead, but then he cracked an eye and saw a man in hunting gear approach through the trees. The man was about thirty years old with a *Semper Fi* tattoo on his forearm.

"Found him, Bowie," the hunter said.

A strong hand pulled his wounded arm over and flipped him onto his back. The sudden movement was so agonizing he clenched his teeth and made an involuntary cry.

"Still alive." The hunter bent over and rifled through Albert's pockets. "Phone, wallet, cabin key, and a car key. How you doin', man?"

"I've been shot," Albert gasped, puffing out the words.

"Yeah, I kind of know that," the hunter said. "I shot you."

"What?" Albert cried and lost consciousness again.

***

Albert returned to the waking world to find himself inside his own nearby cabin, in bed, with a fire blazing in the fireplace. Somebody had covered him with heavy blankets, which were making him shake and sweat at the same time. Bloody bandages lay in a trashcan a few feet away.

The shooter sat in the corner with his dog beside him.

"Who the hell are you?" Albert said, struggling to sit up.

"I'm Derek and this here's Bowie. I shot you, so now I'm going to save your life."

"Save my life!" Albert managed to throw off the blankets. "It wouldn't need saving if you hadn't blown my shoulder to pieces. Give me my phone. I'm calling 911."

"I'm afraid I can't do that," Derek said. "Besides, it's almost nightfall. We've got to change that dressing again, though. I got a first aid kit in my pack."

Almost nightfall. How long had he been out? Too weak to fight, Albert fell back on the pillow. The whole nightmare had to be an accident the hunter wanted to hide from the police.

Derek went into the kitchen, where he moved around and ran the water. Eventually, the man came back into the main room with a paper sack.

Albert had expected him to have a normal medical kit with antiseptic. Instead, Derek pulled out some gauze and tape, the kind you buy in the drugstore, and what looked like tree moss and a Tupperware container full of mud, of all things. Sizing up Albert's wound, he threw away the makeshift bandage he'd put on earlier, plastered the mud and moss all over the bullet hole, and covered the sticky mess with gauze and tape.

Some crazy, homemade redneck remedy.

"Now, we'll keep that on for three days and it should start to scab," Derek said.

"I'm not going to be here for three days," Albert told him.

***

"Shot this rabbit today," Derek said twenty minutes later as he stirred a stew of rabbit, potatoes, carrots, and onions.

Albert's potatoes, carrots, and onions that he'd stocked in the cabin when he checked in. He wondered if the stew would be safe to eat, but the smell of it made his stomach growl. Within a few minutes, the hunter pulled a chair next to the bed and began to try to feed him.

Mortally offended, Albert took the bowl. "I think I can manage to feed myself. Why'd you shoot me?"

Derek stared down at his muddy boots. "By accident. I mistook you for something else."

"Mistook me for what?" Albert said, growing angrier. "I was a man, in a boat, on a lake, in the morning. What do you hunt? Tourists?"

"Look, mister, if I told you, you wouldn't believe me." Derek scraped his chair away from the bed and stood up. "See, it started when I got back from the Middle East last year. All the bombings and killings messed up my head." He looked away. "By the time I came back to the States, I was one drink short of becoming the town drunk. My wife told me to get my shit together or she'd take our kids back to the west coast. So I decided I'd bring my dog and come up here to my uncle's hunting lodge to kick the drinking."

"You have PTSD. For God's sake, go to the VA and get treatment."

"I'm not dealing with those idiots," Derek growled. "I packed up the truck and came up here about a month ago. That's when it started happening."

"What started happening?"

"After about a week up here without the booze, I began sort of seeing things out at the lake." Derek ran his fingers through his high and tight haircut. "Bubbles and shapes in the water."

"I saw the bubbles, too. It's some animal in the lake. Enough of this. I have a car. You drive me to the hospital right now."

Derek picked up Albert's wallet and glanced at the driver's license.

"Well, Albert Salinger, I just can't do that. I can't have you blabbing all over the county that old Derek shot you at Deep Lake."

"I promise not to tell anyone," Albert lied. "Just get me into town or to the town line and I'll be quiet."

"Sorry, no can do."

"You can't keep me a prisoner here," Albert said, staring at the man.

***

Derek threw another log on the fire. The dog circled around on the rug and settled down. While the hunter stared into the flames, Albert lay silently in bed, taking stock of the cabin. His own cabin that he'd rented for the weekend. He didn't even have the key anymore. There was no sign of his car keys, either.

Overpowering Derek might be impossible. If he could wrestle him to the ground and render him unconscious, he could probably get the keys to his car back, but he was injured, smaller than Derek, and an out of shape professor while Derek was a much younger, muscled hunter.

He closed his eyes, no longer able to fend off sleep.

The unnerving howl of a wolf woke him an hour later. His guidebook to the Blue Ridge said black bears, timber wolves, and bobcats roamed the mountains, but nothing could be worse than Derek, who for the moment was nowhere in sight. This was his chance. Maybe he could stumble out to a road and flag somebody down, if he could remember how he'd driven in during the daylight.

He carefully swung his legs over the edge of the bed. His head reeled from the blood loss. Once he made it to his feet, he walked cautiously toward the door and cracked it, hoping Derek had fallen asleep somewhere so he could get away.

Derek was standing at the edge of the lake with his back to the cabin.

"Well, glad to see you're still with the living," Derek said, laughing, his eyes forward.

"You don't miss much, do you?"

"Nope, not since my Marine Corps training. You learn to sleep with your eyes and ears open. You planning on going somewhere?"

"I need to pee. The bathroom door's jammed."

Derek glanced at him and returned his eyes to the lake. "Okay, take your piss and then get back in the cabin. It's not safe out here. I'll kick the door in later."

The lake was as black as midnight under the hills and trees. The moon cast a silver shimmer on the water. Nothing much. Nothing scary. When he'd finished peeing, Albert stood outside for a while, looking around. His rowboat had a gaping hole, undoubtedly thanks to Derek's rifle butt. More ominously, his car was nowhere in sight.

Albert knew next to nothing about weapons, but he spotted a pistol and a rifle on the shore of the lake, alongside what looked like a dozen homemade grenades. All screaming signs that Derek wasn't exactly wound too tight.

"What're you shooting at?" Albert asked, trying to make small talk. Maybe if he could find out more about the hunter, he could figure out what the man had done with his car.

"Never you mind." Derek drew the sleeve of his flannel shirt across his forehead. "Now get back in there or I'll have to blow your foot off for roaming around too much."

Shaking his head, Albert headed back to the cabin, looking over his wounded shoulder before he went inside. Derek was still standing on the edge of the lake as more bubbles rose to the surface.

***

Albert tossed and turned from a feverish fit and finally realized the morning sun was shining down on his bed. He knew he was getting worse and needed to go to a hospital immediately.

When Derek came in with a plate of breakfast, Albert's first thought was to feign disinterest. He knew, though, that a full belly would be better to travel on, if he could just get away.

"Ham and biscuits," Derek said.

Albert almost inhaled the biscuits. "What, no freshly squeezed OJ? You just lost your third star in the guidebooks."

"You're lucky I'm feeding you."

Feeding me with my own food that I brought here. You're lucky I haven't been able to call the cops because that's the last time you'll ever see daylight.

Trying not to stare at the hunter, Albert gingerly moved his arm, positive he'd need surgery, but he was more worried about an infection.

Derek took the empty plate away.

"Get up. We're moving out now." Derek lifted up a backpack that looked like it weighed a hundred pounds. The coonhound was up and ready to go, too.

"Where are we going? Into town?" Albert said, hoping that was true.

"Nope, my uncle's lodge on the other side of the lake. You'll be more comfortable there and I'll be able to keep a better eye on you … and them."

"Who's *them?*" Albert demanded.

"Never mind, just hurry up. We have a lot of ground to cover."

"I have a car. We could drive."

"Why, your gas tank developed a hole. Buy American next time."

Albert bitterly followed Derek and his dog down to the edge of the lake, where they picked up a path filled with stumps and lichen-covered rocks. It was hard going at first, but Albert was surprised to find he could keep up.

After about thirty minutes, though, he slowed down. Derek went ahead. Holding his breath, Albert bent over, and pretended to tie his hiking boot while Derek walked on, apparently unaware of the growing distance between them.

Now or never. Albert bolted into the thick woods as fast as he could. The woods were mostly pines, so his footfalls fell soundlessly on the pine needle covered forest floor. He ran hard for several minutes before he grew so exhausted he had to lean against a tree.

No Derek in sight. Have to keep moving, he told himself. He pushed himself farther into the woods until he came to an old logging road. With his spirits rising, he doggedly followed the road, eager to find a highway or a homestead, anything with people and a phone. Taking a deep breath, he began to jog, thinking he should save his strength instead of run at full speed.

But in a few minutes, Albert's jogging slowed to a fast walk. He was running out of energy fast. Just around the bend in the logging road, he saw the entrance to a paved road. Eureka, he thought.

The lake had to be due east behind him. Never much of an outdoorsman, he followed the road in what he thought was a westerly direction since that was the way the sun was moving.

He walked along that road for quite a while without sight of a single car. Squinting in the sun, he finally made out a service station at the crest of a rugged hill. All he had to do was make it up there and he was home free. After dragging himself up the hill, he reached the service station at last.

Deep Lake Gas and Groceries. His nightmare would be over in a few minutes.

The redheaded teenager behind the counter looked up.

"What can I do for you, mister?" the kid asked.

"I lost my phone. Do you have a phone I can use?" Albert could feel the blood begin to soak through his shirt again.

"I got a phone. Hey, ain't you the guy that got shot yesterday morning?"

"How do you know that?"

"Look, my cousin Derek paid me good money to keep an eye out for you, so you sit tight while I call him."

Albert grabbed a tire iron and waved it recklessly around.

"You do what I say or I'll smash your brains in," he shouted, almost convincing himself he would really do it. "You give me your phone."

The kid stared at him and shook his head.

"You want money?" Albert went on, starting to shake. "I'm filthy rich. I'll pay whatever you want. Call 911 or get me to a hospital."

"Yeah, yeah," the kid said. "Your shoulder's bleeding pretty bad. You better sit down."

The store seemed to spin. Sweat poured from Albert's body. Eventually, he couldn't stand up any longer and collapsed on a beer keg, still holding the tire iron.

"You're not going to help me, are you?" he asked, sighing.

"Well, I'm going to help you get back to Derek, but no, I ain't taking you to no hospital."

Forty minutes passed. Derek finally showed up in a black Dodge truck with the coonhound riding shotgun.

He yelled into the store, "Get your ass in this truck now. We've got to get to the lodge before sundown."

Reluctantly, Albert put the tire iron down, giving the kid one last aggrieved look. He wobbled out of the store and climbed into the truck. The dog growled. By now, he'd lost a lot of blood and felt close to passing out.

***

Back at the lodge, the sun was sinking over the hills, leaving the sky ablaze in a bloody red glow. Loons called from across the still lake. *Red sky at night, sailor's delight*, Albert thought cynically. No sailing or rowing out of this place. Derek had even destroyed his boat.

Once again, Derek stood at the shoreline, staring into the darkening lake.

This time, oddly enough, he'd brought out a folding chair for Albert. Maybe he'd finally realized how serious Albert's injuries had turned out to be.

"What is it you keep waiting for?" Albert asked him point blank.

Derek stared at the water. "You'll see for yourself tonight."

Bubbles rose up to the surface of the lake. Derek fired the gun twice. Albert almost jumped out of his skin as the shell casings fell onto the rocky shore.

"That was one of them," Derek said as he reloaded.

"Why don't you just tell me what they are instead of stringing me along? Fish? Lake monsters?" Albert tried not to laugh.

"I don't know what they are, but I think they followed me here." Derek aimed into the lake again. "Long story short, when I was in the Middle East, I shot these two beggars I thought were suicide bombers always scoping us out. Now I think they really just wanted candy and cigarettes they could sell and whatever money they could scrounge off us, but I blew their heads off. Shoot first and ask questions later, that's my motto. After I took their asses out, I kept thinking they were behind me. I'd turn around real fast, but I could never see them. They were too fast. Sometimes I can still feel them watching me."

"You have PTSD," Albert said. "I told you, go to the VA and get treatment."

"And I told you I'm not dealing with those idiots." Derek fired into the water.

"So you think it's those beggars from the Middle East down in the lake. That's it, isn't it? Ghosts that followed you here. Why, that's totally ridiculous."

"Just you wait."

"Derek, you're screwed up. It's probably a natural phenomenon in the lakebed. You need serious psychiatric help. I can get you that help if you'll just let me go home."

"There's somebody down there and I plan on looking the bastard in the eye before I take him out. And with you here, tonight could be the night I get him."

"I'm not a part of this," Albert said, waving his hands.

"Maybe Mr. Magnum here will convince you otherwise." Derek pointed the pistol at Albert's temple.

Albert slowly leaned back. "You're completely crazy."

The coonhound growled at a sudden rustle in the woods. The dog's fur bristled along its back. Both men stared in the direction of the noise. With his heart pounding, Albert clambered out of his chair, ready to run, while Derek peered through night-vision binoculars at the tree line.

Twigs broke about fifty yards away.

Derek handed him the pistol and whispered, "Shoot at whatever moves."

Albert stared at the gun. Even though it was the first time he'd ever held one, it fit perfectly in his hand. *I could bluff my way out of here with this right now.* He'd never have this chance again. If he didn't act now, he could die out here.

Certain Derek couldn't see him, he carefully lifted the gun to the back of the hunter's head. Before he could think of the next step, low shapes emerged from the shadowy woods. Derek shone the beam of light in their direction.

Three raccoons. The dog raced after them along the shore.

Derek slowly turned around and pressed the barrel of the gun to Albert's forehead. "Now, you man enough to shoot? You go right ahead."

Albert looked him straight in the eyes and felt his hand tremble from the weight of the pistol. Maybe Derek was right. He didn't have the balls after all, a soft, middle-aged man who lived in a college classroom and couldn't even tell east from west. He finally lowered the gun to his side, surprised that Derek didn't rip it out of his hand.

Derek chuckled. "You chickenshit, you."

***

Bigger bubbles rose to the surface of the lake. Ordered by Derek to shoot at the water, Albert took the pistol and emptied it at the bubbles. Derek emptied the rifle and used up all the homemade grenades. The lake lit up like a battlefield.

Silence fell, broken only by the dark waves lapping against the rocky shore.

Derek hadn't reloaded yet. He was out of ammunition. He'd have to go inside the lodge for more bullets.

Albert stared at the hunter. This was his chance to get away. The black water, the night, and the woods might cover him. He couldn't swim far with a bad shoulder, but if he made a break for the trees, maybe he could get away in the dark. Maybe he could lay low until daylight when he'd cross paths with somebody who'd help him.

It might be his only chance. Taking a deep breath, he dashed for the woods along the shore. Seconds later, a knife landed in his calf.

"You knifed me, you bastard," Albert shouted, whirling around. Wincing in agony, he wrenched the knife out of his leg.

Derek pounded closer. "Just keeping you in line. I've got a great arm, man. You're not running away."

The hunter tackled him on the shore. Grunting, they fought for the knife. Sharp rocks dug into Albert's flesh. He had to get away from the maniac. They rolled over and over. Dark water filled Albert's eyes and nose. Derek gripped his neck, squeezing his windpipe. The hunter was too strong. He couldn't fight him off.

They splashed into the lake. Without warning, the lakebed fell sharply away. Water rushed over their heads. A moment from drowning, Albert could smell death all around him. He sucked in a deep breath and held it as they rolled farther into the lake. The hunter still fought him as they fell to the bottom, as if he were taking out all his fury about life on Albert.

Faint moonlight penetrated the murky depths. Albert's feet touched lake slime and silt that coated ancient beer bottles and the hulks of unidentifiable trash people had thrown in the water years before. To his shock, a dim sliver of red light grew across the lakebed as if something knew they'd arrived.

His lungs were about to burst. He couldn't hold on much longer. He would have to breathe soon or die.

And then, with Derek's fists around his neck, he saw the impossible.

A stone arch and stone door lying flat on the lakebed creaked open. The red glow grew wider. Bubbles poured from the doorway. The same bubbles Derek had been obsessed with for days and shooting at with murderous intent.

For a moment, the lake silt formed the words of Dante's *Inferno* over the door, "Abandon all hope ye who enter here," before the waves washed the words away.

Just as Albert's oxygen-starved lungs were about to explode, a horrifying demon climbed from the stone door into the lake. The demon had to be ten feet tall with dark lizard scales and a triangular head with a coral *V* on the crown. It grinned at Derek as if it had been waiting for him and opened its scaly arms in a ghastly embrace. Derek let go of Albert. As the demon and the hunter circled each other, the demon's head shifted from a lizard to the faces of two Middle Eastern beggars with pleading brown eyes. One face appeared, and then the other, as the demon rushed toward Derek.

The two monsters, human and inhuman, grappled with each other in the silt. Easily the master, the demon dragged Derek toward the red door. Bubbles rushed out in a thick column as heat blasted through the water.

Forgotten now, Albert reached out in one last act to save his enemy. In the end, they were both human beings. He grasped for Derek's shirt, trying to keep the demon from dragging him down into the red glow, but the door slammed shut. The stone almost crushed Albert's foot.

Escape. Now. Leave. Run. Go.

Terrified beyond all measure, Albert rose in the water until he broke through the surface. He gasped in huge gulps of air, filling his starved lungs. He had to get out of the lake. He could almost feel the demon's claws on his legs. Every tiny little lie and moment of cowardice and neglect from his whole life came flooding back at him: the piece of candy he stole from a store when he was eight years old, the traffic ticket he never paid, all the times he'd snapped at his parents or forgotten their birthdays. *I'm sorry, I'm sorry, I'm sorry.*

At last, he reached the shore and threw himself upon the rocks.

"No, get up, get up," he screamed at himself.

He couldn't rest. Gasping, he stumbled into the empty lodge. No keys to Derek's truck. The truck was useless. No phone, no wallet, no ID, nothing to prove who he was. He had nothing but his skin and the drenched clothes on his back.

He shook, terrified to stay in the lodge, terrified to run into the night, but he forced himself outside in the direction he thought the road might lie.

The darkness closed around him. Looking back over his wounded shoulder, he spotted the surly coonhound waiting by the lake for the master who would never return. He couldn't help the dog now. He was too injured.

The chilly night air seeped through his wet clothes. He limped along. Soon he began to half-run with his wet hair plastered over his forehead and his arms wrapped around his body. His leg and shoulder were in agony. His smashed foot ached.

He could no longer see the lake, but he knew it was still there, hiding monsters in its depths. The stars shone overhead. Night insects chirred and buzzed. The cries of nature filled the woods, free from the madness of humanity and its horrifying demons.

He turned at a sudden sound.

A long shadow fell over the road behind him. The shadow grew closer, flying toward him with deadly accuracy. Gasping, he ran on ahead. Huge wings glided by his head. This was it then, the end his life … but it only turned out to be an owl. The great bird flew on into the darkness.

Running on raw adrenaline, Albert thudded over the next hill, where he stumbled onto an isolated paved road. He followed the dark road, still looking over his shoulder, until at last he saw the faraway lights of civilization.

He was alone, wounded and soaking wet, but he had survived. He had seen the impossible, but he would live to see tomorrow, his college again, his house and garden, his family and friends. Sobbing, he limped on under the stars, grateful to be alive.

Hell Couch

HA Grant

"We need a couch," Kellie told her boyfriend David. Exhausted from hauling boxes all morning, she pushed her blonde hair away from her face and surveyed the empty living room.

The hundred-year-old townhouse was perfect. It just needed furniture.

"We should get the couch now," she added. "We can always get a rug later on."

David put a box packed with their student papers and textbooks down and crossed his arms over his t-shirt. "Yeah, well, the rent and deposit tapped me out. We'll have to do without a couch for a while, unless you want to go to Furniture World."

Kellie stared at him. "You've got to be kidding."

Ten minutes later, they drove through the downtown Richmond traffic and walked into the cavernous Furniture World warehouse. Kellie rolled her eyes. Ratty World looked more like it. The warehouse had to be the last stop before the dump for every rotten piece of furniture in the city. They poked around musty rooms full of sad, worn-out castoffs for half an hour. Finally, David looked up from a jumble of frayed couches and chairs.

"Look at this one," he said with a triumphant grin.

Kellie stared at the big green couch he'd unearthed.

"That's the ugliest couch I've ever seen in my life," she told him.

"Oh, come on. A couch is a couch."

She shook her head. "It looks like something you'd see in a funeral parlor. I hate the creepy flower pattern. And I hate the color even more."

"What, you don't like bird poop green?"

"Thanks but no thanks. I'd rather sit on the floor."

"No, no, no. We can put a throw over it. Kellie, look, it's solid. It's big. It'll hold a lot of people. And check out the price."

Kellie turned the price tag over. "Only twenty dollars. Well, maybe you're right. Maybe eventually we can hide it with a slipcover. I can't believe we're going to buy this thing."

They paid for the couch and helped an employee wrestle it into the back of Kellie's pickup truck. Then they drove the monstrosity home. It was tough going to get the huge couch into the townhouse. After pushing and pulling it across the porch, they finally managed to shove the couch over the threshold into the living room.

The couch sat in the shadows by the fireplace. Its brooding presence dominated the room, as if it were sizing everything up like a suspicious crocodile. The spiky leaves on the fabric resembled knives or sharp teeth and the flowers looked like multiple pairs of narrowed eyes. Now that the thing was sitting in their house, Kellie really wished they hadn't bought it.

"It's hideous," she said. "And now we've got to buy a throw."

"But look how big it is." David plopped down on the couch. "It's comfortable. You could sleep on it with no problem. The cushions are in good shape, too." He held his hands out. "Come sit with me on our couch."

She shook her head with another skeptical look. "I wonder if we should vacuum it first or use upholstery cleaner. We don't know who else's been sitting there."

"Yeah, good idea." David got to his feet and started to pull up the seat cushions. "Hey look, there's a hole under here. You can see inside."

She grimaced. "Ugh, don't! There could be a mouse in there, or a rat."

"Oh, come on." He laughed.

"You think I'm kidding, but I'm not. Mice like to get inside old furniture."

He leaned over, staring through the big hole in the fabric. "There's something in there all right. I can see it down in the springs."

"Don't put your hand in there. Let me get a flashlight."

"No, don't bother. I've got it." Laughing at her again, David got down on his knees on the bare wood floor and reached his whole arm into the couch.

"What is it?" she asked, barely able to contain her anxiety.

"Not sure. I think I've got it now." He finally pulled his arm back out with a smile. "Look at this, a *wallet*, and it's full of money. A shitload of money."

Dumbfounded, Kellie stared at the ragged black wallet. It bulged with cash.

"Let's just see what we've found," David told her with a smirk, counting out the bills on the back of the couch. "One thousand … two thousand … three … four … five thousand dollars. And you didn't want this couch."

"We can't keep that money, David. We can't keep five thousand dollars."

"Yeah, well, you know I love you, but you can be a do-gooder of the first magnitude. We're keeping it. This is fate coming down on our side."

"No, we can't keep it. Not that much money. Is there an ID in there?"

Frowning, he opened the wallet again. "Yeah, an old driver's license." He pulled it out. "Alfred Redbone."

Kellie stepped around the cushions on the floor to David's side. They gazed at the license together. A man with a shaved head and the cheekbones of a skull stared back at them from the photo.

Alfred Redbone's grim eyes said he'd witnessed more than his share of life's nightmares: the underbelly of abandonment and cruelty, perhaps gangland killings, or the deaths of unwanted children, or the disappearance of whole families in dusty war zones. His skeletal face ended in a slash of a mouth. Worst of all, tattooed letters that spelled "Hell Thing" crawled across his neck.

"God, he's horrible," Kellie said.

David gave a soft whistle. "One nasty bastard."

She took a deep breath. "Well, I don't like the looks of this guy, but we've got to do the right thing. Whoever this Alfred Redbone is, we have to find him and give his money back."

"Nah, I don't think so. We're keeping this money."

"Oh, really?" Kellie retorted, getting mad.

"For two reasons. Number one, nobody walks around with five thousand dollars in their wallet unless they're a drug dealer. Look at his face. I'm not going to knock myself out trying to return five thousand dollars to some lowlife and get robbed for my trouble."

"You don't know that would happen," Kellie began. "And we could mail it."

"What if he's not at that address?" David gave her a knowing look. "And back to reason number two, he's probably dead. People die all the time and leave behind a bunch of junk that nobody wants, so it all ends up in a thrift store. Most of the stuff in thrift stores comes from dead people. Chances are Alfred Redbone's a dealer or he's dead. I say he's dead."

"I'm going to Google him right now." She pulled out her phone.

He laughed. "Sixty-seven Albert Redbones. Every single one's going to claim the money. You really want to take that on?"

She sighed. "I guess not. We should give it back to the store. They're a charity. They'll help poor people with it."

"Yeah, well, we're poor people," he said.

"You're right about that."

"Of course I'm right. I'm right about everything." He kissed her.

She gave him a reluctant kiss back. "Well, I guess we can keep the money then. My truck needs repairs. I worry all the time it's going to break down."

"See? I told you. It's fate. That money's been waiting for us."

She frowned. "But hide it back under the cushions. We don't want it lying around where somebody will see it through the window." She shook her head. "I need coffee."

"Me, too," he said, collecting the cash from the back of the couch.

"I'll find the Keurig." Kellie headed to the kitchen. She still felt a pang of guilt about the money, but her truck did need repairs. Maybe fate really had played a hand. Half the money belonged to David, of course, but maybe he would even agree to a down payment on a new truck, one without rattles and dents. Five thousand would go a long way.

She opened a box. No Keurig. Where did they pack it? Her mind wandered as she opened more boxes. Maybe they could get a couch like the contemporary one with contrasting throw pillows she saw in the mall last week … and a good rug with a Southwestern pattern … and a better kitchen table, one that would seat more than two people.

They'd definitely have to get a new couch … in any color but green.

She found the Keurig.

"Kelleeeeeeee!" David let out a chilling scream that pierced the thick plaster walls of the old townhouse.

She'd never heard him scream like that. She dropped the coffeemaker in the sink and raced down the hall into the living room. He wasn't there. Her heart beat faster as she wheeled around. The couch was the only thing in the room. It sat by the fireplace, surrounded by the cushions on the floor, exactly the way she'd left it two minutes ago.

Except David had been standing there, about to hide the money.

"David?" she called. "Where are you?"

"Uh, uh, uh, uh," he shouted, gasping and panting.

"I can't see you. Where are you?"

"Here! In the couch! Help me, quick!"

She looked around, but still didn't see him.

"Not funny, David. Not cool at all." Shaking her head, she walked up to the couch, expecting to hear his laughter from the hall.

She caught her breath. David's anguished face looked up at her from four or five feet below the seat. Most of the old fabric covering the springs had vanished as if it had melted away. The few remaining shreds blew in an evil, icy wind. Somehow the springs had snapped open in the center like a trapdoor and swung back, resembling two flimsy coiled gates opening into nothingness.

Darkness blacker than black fell away beneath David's running shoes. His body, from his face to his hands to his jeans and pale shoes, looked tiny and lost hanging above that terrible chasm. It was impossible to see what lay below. The impenetrable blackness could have hidden a thousand-foot cavern or even the void of space.

"Oh, my God," Kellie shrieked.

David's eyes implored her to save him. He desperately gripped one side of the gates while his legs dangled and his t-shirt blew in that terrible wind. His other hand held a pile of money. A few hundred-dollar bills escaped his fist, spiraling down into the darkness.

"Help me! Pull me up," he gasped. "I can't hold on!"

She reached in, keeping her knees on the floor for safety, but her arms were too short.

The faint sounds of drums came from far below.

Bone, bone, bone.

It sounded again, over and over, the drums of doom.

Bone, bone, bone.

The living room floor of the old townhouse must have collapsed. The townhouse had to be sitting over a deep sinkhole. Wrenching her eyes away from her boyfriend, Kellie threw herself on the floor so she could peer under the couch. The ordinary wood floor ran undamaged all the way to the walls. There was no hole anywhere.

The black pit wasn't below the townhouse.

It was inside the couch.

"That's impossible," she cried, kneeling in front of the couch with her blood roaring in her ears. David was still hanging on, swinging over the chasm, his fingers turning white from gripping the coiled gate.

"Kellie, do something!" He tried to pull himself up, but couldn't get anywhere.

Those horrible drums throbbed in the depths.

Bone, bone, bone.

"I'm going to save you, I swear." Her voice shook as she leaned even farther over the chasm. Her arms were still too short. Much too short. "I can't reach you. I'm calling 911."

His face grew more desperate. "There's no time. Pull me up."

"I can't reach you, David!" She grabbed her phone and punched 911. "My boyfriend fell … I don't know if he's hurt … He fell inside the couch … No, damn you, this is not a prank! They hung up on me! 911 hung up on me!"

"Throw me something," he screamed. "Rope! Curtains!"

"We don't have rope or curtains," she screamed back.

"Come on, Kellie! Pull me up."

"I can't," she wailed, but she climbed up on the edge of the couch, trying to balance herself over the vast black hole.

Bone, bone, bone.

"Come on, Kellie! Come on, pull me up!"

"I can't, I can't," she gasped, stretching her arms out as she leaned almost her whole body over the black pit. She tried to hook her sneakers under the couch, but her feet slipped on the wood floor.

"I've almost got your hand," he said. "I got it! I got it! Now pull me up!"

"I can't, David, I can't …. Wait, don't pull me, don't …. Daaaaaaaaaavid."

***

Tom Harvey stepped over the pile of mail scattered across the foyer. College students could be a complete pain.

"Yeah, that's right," he said into his cell phone. "So you've got the address … Yeah, a couple of students skipped out on the rent and left their furniture … Yeah, they've been gone for a while, haven't picked up their mail in weeks. It's all over the floor inside the front door … What've I got? A queen-sized bed, dresser, kitchen table and two chairs, and oh, yeah, a big couch. When can you pick it up? … You're in the area now? … What, thirty minutes? Say, that's great. I'll be here."

He put his phone away and walked through the deserted townhouse into the living room, where he stared out the window, just in case. No sign of the Furniture World truck yet.

"Students." He shook his head. "Either trashing the place or skipping out on the rent. It never ends."

He checked his phone again. Twenty-eight minutes until the truck showed up. Well, he wasn't going to stand the whole time. Looking for a place to sit down, he sized up the old green couch. It was the only piece of furniture in the living room.

Now that he had time on his hands, he took a good long look at the couch. It had to be the ugliest piece of furniture he'd ever come across. And that was after ten years of hauling away crappy old couches and chairs the students always left behind in his rentals. The terrible fabric on this dog of a couch had a morbid flower pattern that reminded him of a funeral parlor or an old ruined bouquet in a graveyard.

He blinked. The spikes on the flowers resembled knives, of all things. Somebody had a sick sense of humor making a damn pattern like that.

The landlord wasn't an imaginative man, though. Not at all. In the end, it was just an old couch. The sooner he got rid of it, the better. He shrugged off the strange thoughts and checked his phone again. Twenty-five minutes to go.

"Might as well sit down," he said.

He crossed the bare living room floor and sat down on the couch to wait.

The Wreck of U-913 and Other Dark Tales (Vol. 2)

The Wreck of U-913

AC Stone

I hated the silence of the descent. Sure, there were sonar pings, and the captain reported our position and the external pressure every few minutes. Mostly we said nothing to each other as the deep-sea submersible *Titus-IV* left the sunlight zone and glided into the dark void of the abyss. The titanium hull groaned against the constantly increasing water pressure. You'd think that I'd be used to it after eleven dives hunting for treasure, but I wasn't. The long silences let your imagination wander and reminded you that no one should be this far below the surface. Just nerves, I guessed. You needed them to stay focused.

When I put on my atmospheric diving suit, I'd be in control. Aboard this submersible, I was just cargo. Today would be new territory: a sunken Nazi submarine just beyond the edge of the continental shelf. The wreck was at a depth of about 760 meters, near the outer tolerance limit of my suit. The risk would be worth it, if U-913 was actually full of stolen gold and somehow we all got back safely. Everything had to go just right. There's no forgiveness at the bottom of the ocean.

I leaned over toward Bill Jansen, the engineer seated across from me in the back of the submersible, and said, "These descents take forever."

"Yeah," he replied, switching his toothpick to the other side of his mouth.

"But the slower, the safer. We'll catch a problem and have a shot at fixing it … or haul this bucket back to the surface."

"Still, almost forty minutes to reach bottom."

"What are you complaining about? You got the window seat."

An acrylic porthole six inches thick offered a view into total blackness. The propellers hummed a low and steady drone. I unwrapped a stick of cinnamon gum and popped it into my mouth. I offered a piece to Bill, but he waved it off.

Captain Theresa Apfeld's voice came over the intercom. Like everyone else on our submersible, she went by her first name, which was kind of cool. Theresa contacted our support ship on the surface. "*Calisanya*, do you copy? Over."

The radioman replied, "Copy, *Titus-IV*. Over."

A long buzz of static. Then a sharp crackle over the speakers made us wince.

The radioman on the *Calisanya* repeated that he was there.

Theresa said, "Sorry. Some issue with the radio, but we're fine. Past 500 meters. All systems go. Over."

"Acknowledged, *Titus-IV*. You're about eighty meters starboard of the wreck. Start to compensate. Over."

"The currents down here are stronger than anticipated," Theresa replied. "I was keeping away from the edge of that steep canyon. Initiating correction."

"Okay. Report back at 700. Over."

"Roger that. We'll just about be there. *Titus-IV* out."

Radio static began again.

Theresa said, "Bill, check out communications. Something's wrong. I'm not getting called back up over a radio on the fritz."

"I'm on it." Bill unfastened his shoulder straps and crawled forward to the cockpit with the captain and navigator.

I was alone in the back of *Titus-IV*.

Bill returned in a few minutes, running his thick fingers through his crewcut. "Couldn't find anything wrong with the radio. The static stopped on its own. Weird. First we got these strong currents nobody knew about and now the radio's acting up."

"Yeah, weird," I replied.

Bill started to fasten his shoulder straps, then apparently thought otherwise. "So you shot down my first theory why the U-boat sank."

"Come on," I said with a shrug. "If it were too heavy with gold, it would've slammed into the bottom of the Hamburg harbor, which would've been amusing. U-913 made it here almost to the coast of Argentina."

"And my second theory about running out of fuel doesn't work."

"They'd have waited at the surface for a rescue. Besides, these subs had good range, so only one refueling was needed. German supply tankers were in the Atlantic for at least two weeks after the surrender. A supply ship could have thought U-913 was headed back to Europe. On the other hand, a submarine full of gold and torpedoes could've bribed or threatened any ship on the high seas for more fuel."

"Makes sense. Anyway, the U-boat sank here. Somehow they refueled. And no allied attack either. There'd be a record. I guess it's a mystery."

The sonar system pinged. I could hear the navigator, Yasui Kunitaro, whispering to the captain, but I couldn't make out what he was saying.

Bill grabbed his toothpick, pointed at me casually, and asked, "So, you got it figured out, huh?"

"No, just a theory of sorts. The U-boat crew and their Gestapo passengers had only a day or so before reaching Buenos Aires with pallets of gold bars. If the Gestapo didn't want to share, they might've murdered the crew, or at least most of them. Kept a few alive at gunpoint to pilot the sub. Or maybe the crew mutinied to take the gold from the Gestapo. Went on their own little killing spree. A submarine loaded with fuel tanks and torpedoes is no place for a gunfight, but that could explain how they got all the way across the Atlantic only to sink in relatively safe waters off South America."

"Maybe … maybe," Bill replied. "Gold makes people do strange things. You know there could be half a billion dollars in gold on U-913 … today's money, of course."

"A lot back in 1945, too."

"If you're right, those Nazis dropped down to the abyss fighting over all that gold." Bill smiled, showing his teeth.

"Yeah," I said. "Never to see the surface again. No one'll ever know for sure."

Bill chomped on his toothpick and leaned back into his chair. "You'll do fine down there. Just like crackin' a safe, except in total darkness at the bottom of the sea."

Titus-IV turned abruptly, listing toward the port side of the submersible.

Bill grasped his armrests, clicked the buckles of his shoulder restraints, and said, "Whatever you do while you're out there, keep that tether connected to *Titus-IV*."

"I know the protocols."

He nodded and pressed a white button beneath the monitor. "We should be able to get a clear sonar picture of the sub now."

The false-color image of the U-boat appeared on the video screen in shades of yellow and orange against the blue background of the ocean floor. The submarine rested on its side, so we had a detailed view in profile. The hull was intact, without any obvious holes to prove that an explosion had dragged U-913 to the bottom. The periscope and anti-aircraft gun were still atop the conning tower. Bill adjusted his joystick until he located the huge propeller.

"Well, Marcus, there she is," Bill said. "And in near perfect condition."

"Amazing," I replied. "Are we too far away to see it with the regular cameras?"

"Yeah, probably, but I'll try." Bill fidgeted with the switches and buttons around the monitor. The screen turned dark, except for two columns of light from *Titus-IV* that extended downward into the blackness. "Nah, the search lights don't reach yet."

"Zoom into the direction of the U-boat, you know, where you located it with the sonar. It'll come into view in a few minutes. I want to be the first to actually see it."

"Okay," Bill said, chuckling at me a bit.

The columns of light faded until the screen was totally dark. Bill pressed the joystick forward to focus on the exact location of U-913. About a dozen small, distinct lights appeared on the video screen. The glowing lights were moving.

"What the hell are those?" Bill asked, trying to zoom in even closer.

The camera lens reached its maximum resolution, but the lights kept moving away.

"Just pick one of those things and stay with it," I suggested.

"All right," Bill said, "but it ain't easy."

He attempted to track a single glowing light, but it crept off and drifted out of the picture. He kept trying.

"Don't really look or move like fish, you know, with bioluminescence," I said.

"No, they appear almost … spiny."

"Yeah, like giant crabs or lobsters or something."

Bill snorted. "Not seen anything like that before. They're fast."

"And big."

"Hard to tell without a better frame of reference. For us to see bioluminescence from this distance, well, yeah … they're big."

"What do you think?" I asked him.

"About five or six feet. Maybe more. Not sure this far away."

I tried to decipher what was on the video screen, but was at a loss. A strange thing about the ocean is that it covers over seventy percent of the Earth, but nobody really knows that much about it. Less than two percent of the abyss has been explored, if that. We know more about the surface of the moon that we do the deep ocean. We certainly haven't discovered everything that lives down here. I had no idea what those things were.

Bill said, "I can't stay on them. Keep scurrying off. Probably all over that U-boat. We'll get a better look when we're closer."

Theresa's voice came through our headsets. "*Calisanya*, come in."

The radioman replied, "*Calisanya* here, Captain. Over."

"Approaching 700 meters. I got U-913 on sonar. We're just above it. Over."

The radioman paused and exhaled. "Our system confirms your position. Slow for final descent. Over."

"Roger that."

Bill moved the microphone on his headset toward his mouth and interrupted Theresa. "Hey, um, we got something on the U-boat. Something alive."

"What?" Theresa asked from the cockpit. "Hang on. I'm on with the support ship."

Bill said, "There's something crawling on U-913. We should check it out."

Theresa replied, "I have the U-boat on sonar in high resolution. There's nothing there. What're you talkin' about, Bill?"

"Standing-by, *Titus-IV*," the radioman on the surface said without concealing much annoyance.

"Sorry, *Calisanya*, be back with you in a sec," Theresa said. "Bill, what's going on?"

"Well, not sure," he replied. "Look at the digital cameras, not sonar. Bioluminescence. Something's fairly big down there."

"The sonar would detect any large marine life," Theresa said. "Nothing's there."

"There're about a dozen, um, glowing things on U-913 right now. Not in focus. Switch to Digital Camera 2. You'll see 'em."

"Not now, Bill," Theresa said. "These currents are pushing us around, and I need to navigate us in close. Give me a few."

The radioman on our support ship said, "*Titus-IV*, status report?"

Theresa responded, "Just about there. Fifty-one meters to target. Hull pressure stable. Oxygen in the green zone. Batteries at eighty-nine percent. The crew's a go. I'd say we've made it. Over."

"Roger that," the radioman said. "Good job and happy hunting. Over."

I turned to Bill. "What if the support ship scans the wreck for those glowing things?"

Bill Jansen frowned at me, and I realized it was a dumb suggestion on my part. *Calisanya* was more than the height of the Empire State Building above us on the surface. Its sonar couldn't pick up the details we were seeing.

Theresa said, "We'll go around and do a survey of the entire U-boat. Bill, are you sure you saw something?"

"Yeah, crawling on the wreck. Fairly large. Glowing with bioluminescence. Very cool. We got to check 'em out."

Our headphones buzzed with static, a low growl that gradually increased in volume, then faded, and grew louder again before stopping.

Bill said apologetically, "Hey, listen, everyone. I got no idea what's with the radio. Annoying, for sure, but let's get through this and I'll fix it back on the surface. All right?"

Our navigator, Yasui, said, "Bill, when the static started, we had an eleven percent drop in battery power. Now it's back."

Bill Jansen turned sharply toward his instrument panel. "Batteries don't just recharge themselves. Just a temporary gauge malfunction. We're fine, and think about it. We're in reach of all that gold. Magnetic fields can cause this kind of interference. No worries. I'll keep an eye on it."

On the video screens, the spiny, glowing lights on the hull of the U-boat had disappeared.

"Hey, Bill," I said. "Those things are gone."

"What do you mean gone?"

"Just that. Gone."

He adjusted his joystick that controlled the digital cameras, frowned, and said nothing as the monitors remained dark, without the glowing lights moving on them anymore.

Theresa said, "We're close to the wreck. Our search lights or the sound of our propellers might've scared them off. Starting a full survey of the wreck, stern to bow. We'll take it nice and slow and see what's here."

The tiny portholes didn't offer much of a view, but in turn we pressed our faces on the thick clear plastic to see the wreck with our own eyes. The dual search lights illuminated the hull. For the first time in nearly a century, light shone on the sunken U-boat. The sonar image we captured during our descent had given me the impression that the submarine was in good condition, but the search lights offered a different perspective. The metal was deteriorating along every surface, which was encrusted with a film of silt that appeared almost fuzzy. Some of the welded seams held fast, but others had split open, exposing dark crevices into which our search lights couldn't penetrate. Dull orange rusticles hung like stalactites from the edges of the propeller and conning tower. The once-powerful U-913 rested in haunting stillness as beams of light passed over its features in silence. Long shadows blended into the total blackness behind the crumbling wreck.

Titus-IV lurched hard to the side, pushing me against the wall of the cramped submersible.

"Hang on," Theresa said. "These currents must be coming up from that steep canyon beyond the wreck site. Sorry, but no way to predict them." She stabilized our craft with a sharp turn of her steering column and maneuvered us to face the side of the U-boat we hadn't yet explored.

She said to our engineer, "Systems check."

Bill replied with an uncharacteristically official tone for him, "Oxygen, seven hours remaining. Electrical, same. Seven hours. Life support within safe parameters. Propulsion, check. All systems good."

Theresa said, "Are you guys sure you saw something alive on the U-boat?"

Bill turned to me, an expression of mild uncertainty across his face.

I said, "Yes. Definitely. You saw them too, Bill."

"Yeah," he replied cautiously, as if he were mulling over his memory, doubting himself. "Yeah, I did."

Theresa piloted *Titus-IV* along the edge of U-913 where it rested on the ocean floor, giving us a clear view of the top of the U-boat. When she reached the stern, she simply said, "Well, that's it. Both sides. There's nothing alive here whatsoever."

I couldn't argue with her. The submarine wreck was as lifeless as an abandoned morgue.

Theresa said, "We're going back about twenty yards to that big hole near the stern of the U-boat. Could be your entry point, Marcus."

It would be easier for me to get inside through a hole blown through the hull than squeezing through the top-hatch in an atmospheric diving suit, assuming I could even get a hatch open after so many decades. At least this was some good news, depending on the size of the opening and the stability of the hull around it. Theresa glided *Titus-IV* into position near the gaping hole in the lower side of the submarine. The sheet metal was blown outwards with jagged crusts of steel extending around the edges. The torpedoes were in the bow of the sub, but this explosion happened near the stern where the diesel fuel tanks would have been.

Bill the engineer said, "Hey, look there, Marcus. You might be right. The fuel tanks blew up from the inside. Could've been gunfire."

"Maybe," I said, scanning the video screen for those glowing lights we had seen crawling on the wreck when we first approached, but I saw nothing.

"That hole is almost buried in the mucky bottom, so you'll have to crawl into it, but it's the best entry point I saw. You up for it, Marcus?"

"You bet. As long as I can get in and out." I didn't want to think about the hull rolling on its side even a few feet and sealing me inside the wreckage. "I'll check it out."

"Okay then," Theresa said plainly. "Time for you to suit up."

I pressed through a hatch into the cramped transition chamber that held my atmospheric diving suit. I reached above my head, grabbed a crossbar, and did a half chin-up so I could slip my legs down into the lower half of the bulky yellow aluminum suit. Bill lowered the top half of the suit onto me as I slid my arms into place and stood up straight, adjusting my body until I could see through the clear plastic helmet. Bill secured the top and bottom halves of the suit together. The computer automatically sealed the seam around my waist airtight, which the diagnostic computer program confirmed in a mechanical voice over my headphones. I was ready to start the transition that would allow me to enter the enormous, crushing pressure of the water at the bottom of the sea.

"Okay, kid," Bill said, his voice tentative in my headphones. He tapped the shoulder of my suit as some kind of encouragement, which I heard but didn't feel. "You'll like this new microphone I added. Sounds around you will transmit over your radio. I'll get the water pressure equalized inside and out. Then it's all you."

Bill stepped out and spun the hatch wheel until a red light on the wall turned green. Alone in the transition chamber, I controlled my breathing, cleared my head, and thought about how the hatch wheel reminded me of a bank vault back in my hometown, or at least that place I used to call my hometown a long time ago. My mother didn't get a lot of child support from my dad, who left us when I was maybe two or three. When she did get a check from him, we went straight to a bank with a shiny vault that had a wheel like the hatch to this transition chamber. I never visited that bank again after my mother died from ovarian cancer. I don't remember my father's face at all, and I can barely recall what my mother looked like. It's strange, but I can visualize that wheel on that bank vault clearly in my mind after all these years. What you remember and what you forget doesn't always make sense.

I was isolated from the main chamber of *Titus-IV* that held the rest of the crew. After what seemed like a long time, Bill's voice came through my headphones. "You ready?"

"Let's do it."

The floor filled with water from the tanks that lined the transition chamber. The air pumped out of the cramped room as the water level rose until I was completely submerged. The pumps that pressurized the water had to run for seventeen minutes, give or take.

I don't really know what drew me to this line of work. For the crew of *Calisanya*, it was treasure and riches. Sure, the money would be great, but maybe I had different motives. Exploring new worlds and stepping out into the darkness of the ocean floor was pure adrenaline. I was addicted to the rush – always have been. Parachuting on my eighteenth birthday. Rock climbing. Base jumping. But this was even better. To step into the bleak desertlike conditions of the dark abyss jolts your core. No one had ever been to this deep location before now – except I guess for those drowning German sailors who went down with U-913. But unlike them, I was coming back. Perhaps that was it more than anything else. If I had to be honest with myself, walking on the edge of death, being alone in those cold canyons of darkness, and then coming back alive had to be the coolest thing I had ever experienced.

Bill said the pressure inside the transition chamber matched the water pressure outside *Titus-IV*. He opened a series of vents, gradually mixing the exterior water with that inside the transition chamber. I grabbed the stainless steel pry-bar with a wide scoop on the end, the only tool I would have outside the submersible. The lights encircling the rim of the outer hatch dimmed so my eyes could adjust. With a sharp tug, I ensured the tether line that connected me to *Titus-IV* held firm, and then I checked again to be sure, harder this time. I depressed a lever that opened the exterior hatch and stepped out into the abyss.

The absolute blackness felt more like a huge wall pressing in on you than what it actually was: a vast expanse of void. My feet sank a bit into the slick sediment of the bottom, not exactly sand, but more like a sludgy mud. Water currents shoved me toward my left side, but I kept my balance. The currents drifted across the new microphone that Bill had installed. The swirling waters sounded like an icy wind blowing through a forest of barren trees. I kind of wanted Bill to mute the exterior microphone, but I figured that I'd keep it on.

The searchlights from *Titus-IV* provided a straight line to the hole in the U-boat. The top of U-913 faced me, and up close my helmet lights illuminated the rusting, deteriorating metal plates. Somehow the long submarine reminded me of a giant building that had fallen on its side, resting oddly yet firmly on the ocean floor. Where the beams of light could no longer reach, the U-boat hull faded into total darkness.

Our navigator, Yasui, said into my headphones, "Respiration and heart rate are increasing." With *Titus-IV* hovering in place, he had changed his role to monitor my vital signs.

No kidding, I thought. My blood pressure, as well. I figured that Yasui was just trying to prove he was still relevant to the mission while *Titus-IV* was stationary. I simply replied, "I'm good."

"Roger that."

The hole at the stern of the submarine was large, jagged, and partly buried in the ocean floor. I wasn't sure I could squeeze through it in my diving suit. I knelt down and angled the lights on my diving helmet to see inside. The interior was what I'd expected, a dark and empty room with no movement of anything at all except some drifting detritus that I must have kicked up. To get my bulky suit through, I would have to enlarge the opening by digging out some of the sediment.

"We see what you see on our video," Bill said. "Clear away that muck and you'll get in."

Theresa said, "Marcus, if your tether line gets caught up while you're in there or if you have to disconnect for any reason, right here is our meeting point. No matter what, we'll pick you up here."

"Got it. Rendezvous confirmed. Over."

I dug into the sediment with the scoop end of my pry-bar and enlarged the hole until it looked like I could fit through it.

Bill said, "Just remember, Marcus, that's ten thousand years of whale crap you're shoveling."

"Keep it up, man, and I'll bring you back some as a souvenir."

Theresa and Yasui waved cautiously from behind the thick plastic portholes of *Titus-IV*. Their searchlights nearly blinding me, I squinted and turned back toward U-913 so my eyes could readjust. I scanned inside the hole and then the length of the sunken Nazi submarine. Those glowing spiny things were nowhere to be found.

"I'm heading in."

The hull of the U-boat was layered with several dense sheets of curved metal which were separating and rusting. I squeezed through the gap on all fours, churning up sludge that clouded the water around me. Only the sound of my breathing broke the silence. My helmet lights were useless facing downward, but I pressed forward until I cleared the hole and angled my way into an expansive room with a network of pipes along the walls. Some of the pipes were intact while others were bent and crushed near what I thought were the long rectangular diesel engines, now covered in spots by fine silt that must have slipped through the cracks above me. My lights gave the entire chamber an oddly pale blue-green glow. My escape route behind me was not shrouded in darkness, as a result of the glare from the searchlights of *Titus-IV*.

The explosion had definitely originated from the fuel tanks in the stern. Torn fragments of metal barrels rested on the floor of the sideways submarine. I guessed I wasn't walking on the floor, but actually a wall. Additional fuel tanks in the engine room could have helped transport the sailors across the Atlantic to their new lives in South America, but all that extra fuel was dangerous. If I'd had more time, I might have been able to figure out what caused the blast that had dragged U-913 and its crew to the bottom. Mechanical failure? A careless cigarette? Poorly stored fuel barrels? A gunfight between the crew over more stolen gold than anyone could imagine? I sifted through the junk with the robotic fingers of my dive suit and discarded a long crescent wrench that clanged dully when it struck the metal beneath me. No gold bars were anywhere in the engine room, just the corroding debris of the wreck.

Theresa said, "Come in, Marcus. Give us a status. Over."

"Copy that. Nothing in the engine room." I arced my helmet lights to scan above me. The ceiling was actually the opposite wall of the sunken wreck that rested on its side. To my left, the lights reached a far bulkhead toward the center of U-913. The hatch was closed, the light fixtures shattered, the fire hose coiled on a large metal spool.

"No," Theresa said. "I meant you. Over."

"Well, I'm fine." The lighted displays at the base of my helmet near my chin showed the water temperature, water pressure, battery power, body temperature and the remaining oxygen in my tanks. "I'm good for another sixty minutes. All systems green."

"Pulse and respiration still elevated," Yasui said, but I ignored him. The hatch to the next chamber was in reach if I cleared my tether line from the edge of the hole in the hull.

I trudged over the cluttered floor, stepping over tools and shards of metal that the explosion had shredded. I slowly and gently pulled the tether line behind me until I had enough slack to go farther into the wreck.

Bill said, "Great pictures, Marcus. If you come up empty on the stolen loot, then we can cash in on the video."

"Works for me. We're pretty far afield from the original purpose of *Titus-IV* and this suit." The first three Titus-class submersibles were designed for multinational petroleum companies to service oil rigs and prevent another massive spill like the Deepwater Horizon accident in the Gulf of Mexico. The sale of those three submersibles and the atmospheric dive suits had given us enough money to build our own setup and explore the ocean for treasure that no one could reach before now.

"Yeah, kid, but that hatch door probably won't open. Not after all these decades."

"I'll see what the pry-bar can do."

"It's not leverage on the hatch wheel. It's the different water pressures between the chambers."

Bill was almost certainly right. For the first time after I had entered the shell of what was once the deadly U-913, I considered the possibility that I might come back emptyhanded, with just the ordinary junk that German sailors would have kept, and not hundreds of millions of dollars in gold that our research had suggested was here. Seven weeks aboard *Calisanya* conducting wide sonar sweeps off Argentina until we located the lost Nazi sub, now maybe all for nothing.

"I'm going to give it a try, but I could use a little more tether line to get farther in. Theresa, how about moving a little closer? Over."

"No way, Marcus," Theresa said. "You're forgetting the currents that are throwing us around out here. Can't risk it. Over."

"I could disconnect and go on." Even I knew that was a terrible idea, but I really just wanted to get Theresa to move *Titus-IV* closer to the wreck and give me a few more yards of slack.

The silence on the other end of the radio gave me pause. Maybe they were okay with me disconnecting the tether line that kept me anchored to *Titus-IV* so I could continue searching for the gold. I inhaled and exhaled, waiting.

Eventually Theresa said, "No. Just go as far as you can and then report back. Over."

"Hey, Bill. You keeping an eye out for me?"

"Yeah, watching your video feed, but also scanning the exterior hull and the perimeter with sonar. There's nothing moving around out there. You're good. Over."

"All right. I'll try the hatch."

I inserted my pry-bar into the hatch wheel, but before I could yank it to see if it would spin, the door shifted and swung open. "Not shut when the sub went down."

Bill replied, "Yeah, then the whole thing flooded fast and dropped like a stone. Good news is you can get through."

"If I got enough line." The radio started to crackle with a low static buzz that increased in volume and then faded.

My atmospheric diving suit wouldn't go through the hatch. I tried sideways and then headfirst, but the circumference was too wide to fit through the narrow oval. There was no going farther.

If the U-boat had split into pieces back in 1945, we could just pick up the treasure on the ocean floor, but somehow the submarine remained together as it descended into this cold, watery wasteland. Whatever was inside the vessel would likely remain there. My helmet lights let me peer into the next chamber, even though I could not go inside.

I had difficulty orienting myself to the long, narrow room that lay sideways. At first, I thought I was looking at rows of shelves, but realized they were the metal frameworks of bunk beds. There were three oddly shaped protrusions on the wall to my left, which had to be antique toilets near some shadowy recesses that might have been shower stalls. The living quarters for the sailors seemed tight and cramped.

"Hey Bill," I asked. "How many people would have been on a U-boat like this?"

"A full crew would have totaled forty-one, but that wasn't the case here. Most of the sailors were accounted for after Germany surrendered. As best we can tell, U-913 left with only thirteen crew members along with five high-ranking Gestapo officers. Would've been eighteen people on board when it sank. Over."

"Not enough to cross the ocean safely, huh?"

Bill exhaled audibly over my headset. "Obviously." I imagined him shaking his head.

"Have you noticed what's unusual here?" I asked him.

"Everything looks unusual where you're at now, Marcus."

"All those people on board. Well, I figured I'd find some skulls or bones or something."

"Huh," Bill grunted. "Guess you're right. None at all."

My helmet lights illuminated the sleeping quarters all the way to the next bulkhead, but it didn't matter since I was out of tether line. No bones at all. I was nearly finished peering inside when I noticed something strange among the bunks of the sideways submarine. Piles of rocks or boxes, or maybe something else altogether, had collected randomly around the rusting bunk frames. The piles were covered in muck and sediment like everything inside this wreck, but the forms were rectangular and uniform. They were bricks, and all just beyond my grasp. I extended my body as far as I could and reached the pry-bar into the sleeping quarters. One or two bricks were close enough for the pry-bar to touch them, but the angle wasn't good. After a few attempts, I dragged the closest brick toward me. The robotic fingers of the diving suit had difficulty picking up the oddly heavy brick, but I soon held it firmly and scraped away the layer of crusty sediment that encased it. Even in the artificial light cast from my helmet, I could tell it was pure gold.

"Come in, *Titus-IV*. Theresa ..."

Before I could say anything more, the crew of *Titus-IV* was whooping and cheering. I guess in all the excitement, I forgot that they were watching me discover the gold bar in real time on their video monitors.

I said, "I'm bringing this little beauty back right now."

I stepped over the corroding debris in the engine room to the hole in the hull that *Titus-IV* still illuminated. I still was not used to crawling through a hole in this bulky atmospheric diving suit, but I managed. Back at our submersible, I placed the first gold bar inside the water-filled transition chamber, but I stayed outside.

"Theresa," I said. "I've enough battery power to go back in. At least thirty minutes."

"That's too tight," she replied disapprovingly. "We know we can do this right, so let's take our time, come back with a longer tether, and really haul out the treasure. One gold bar is good for now."

"Aw, come on, Theresa," Bill whined. "Just one? We're this far and it only took him a few minutes to get back to us. One more run. What'd ya say?"

Yasui said, "I think it would be okay. Besides, there's limited room for cargo in the transition chamber. The more we bring each trip, the better."

"All right," Theresa said, but I could tell it was against her better judgment. "Just a fast in and out, Marcus. Then we're back to the surface."

I quickly returned to U-913, well, as quickly as anyone could move in this diving suit, heading directly to the spot where I found the first gold bar. Before reaching out to grab another one, I angled my lights to see how many gold bars had fallen into jumbled mounds when the U-boat sank. I wasn't the best at guessing, but I figured there might be thousands of bars of stolen Nazi gold. We hadn't even explored the remaining chambers of U-913 yet.

I snatched up a second bar of gold, and static over my headphones roared in my ears and then ceased. The battery icon inside the base of my helmet flashed, showing that I had just experienced a twenty percent drop in the power needed to heat my dive suit and circulate oxygen. My microphone detected something that sounded like jagged rocks being scraped against the rusting exterior of the submarine. Yellow-green lights appeared through the cracks in the separating metal plates above me, casting columns of light that were filled with drifting flecks of detritus that reminded me of dust. The scraping sound grew louder and came from directions all around me. The eerie lights grew brighter in spots and darker in others, shifting in intensity and color from yellow to green to violet. The gold bar slipped from the robotic hands of my dive suit. Something alive was moving above me.

"Marcus! Get back here," Theresa yelled.

There is no sprinting in a bulky atmospheric diving suit at the bottom of the sea, but I followed the tether line hand-over-hand as fast as I could until I reached the hole where I had entered the wreck.

"What is it?" I asked.

"Get back here. We're losing power."

If they lost electrical power, they would have to release the ballast in order to rise to the surface, which is the most dangerous way to ascend.

"What's going on?" I asked.

Bill said, "They're all over the sub, Marcus. About twenty of them. I don't know. Get back here now."

I crawled through the hole in the hull. The darkness outside the U-boat was filled with glowing skeletal figures made from human bones and skulls, but they were hunched over as if the water pressure had twisted and contorted them into the shapes of crustaceans. They scurried over the surface of the U-boat on all fours, creeping quickly over the ocean floor, moving toward *Titus-*

IV as it hovered in place. The bones flashed and glowed like the shifting neon colors of bioluminescent creatures from the deepest abyss.

I staggered backwards, trying to process what I was seeing.

"Come on," Yasui implored me.

Some of the glowing skeletons reached the stern of *Titus-IV* and clawed at the transition chamber where I had left the first bar of gold. One of the yellow-green skeletons was directly between me and our submersible, so I came up behind it and swung my pry-bar as hard as I could. The pry-bar passed through it as if nothing was there.

The ghost skeletons leaped onto the surface of *Titus-IV*, scratching at the hull, scampering on it from bottom to top, seeking a way inside. Then one skeleton creature seemed to melt slowly into the hull of the submersible and disappeared.

Yasui screamed, followed by Theresa. I heard thrashing sounds and howls through my headset. Finally, Bill released a high, agonizing screech.

Then, all the screaming stopped.

Titus-IV veered away from me violently, yanking me off my feet by the tether line and dragging me across the ocean floor away from the wreck. Our submersible turned sharply, slammed into the bottom, and rolled as if no one piloted the helm anymore. The propellers, visible in the glow of the search lights, moved *Titus-IV* randomly until it dipped downward and disappeared over the edge of the canyon. I had to act instantly. There was no choice, if I didn't want to follow them down into the abyss. I disengaged the tether line as their search lights faded away completely. Now only my helmet lights illuminated the total darkness of the ocean floor around me.

They'd come back. They had to. They'd recover and find a way to get me. I called out, "*Titus-IV*, come in."

There was no reply.

"Theresa? Yasui?"

The sound of my panicked breathing filled my helmet.

"Bill?"

Only silence.

The rendezvous point. I had to get back to that hole in U-913. It was my only chance. Without *Titus-IV*, I had no way to return to the surface. Theresa said she'd pick me up there, no matter what. The U-boat was not visible anywhere in the darkness around me. I had been dragged too far.

The voice of the computer in the atmospheric suit said, "Life support remaining: Eleven minutes. Correction: Eight minutes."

The display icons for power and oxygen at the base of my helmet flashed red. Something was rapidly draining the battery that heated my diving suit and circulated oxygen. The computer voice again ordered me to return to *Titus-IV* immediately. Radio static buzzed in my ears like thousands of insect wings. I started to hyperventilate, which is the worst thing you can do on a dive. I tried to control my breathing, but wasn't successful. My pulse throbbed in my neck and forehead.

Water currents carried away the cloudy water around me until I could see as far as my helmet lights would allow. Two lights appeared in the distance, moving toward me, growing larger and more defined.

"*Titus-IV*, come in. I'm over here. I see you."

No response.

"Over here!"

The lights were almost upon me, but they were not searchlights. Yellow-green shapes materialized fully, flashing and shimmering like the bioluminescent creatures of the deep sea. Glowing bones and skulls formed distinctly in the dark waters, human-shaped skeletons that were hunched over and crawling on all fours like crabs that surrounded me. When my helmet lights shone directly on them, they disappeared. My lights showed only detritus drifting through the water. In my peripheral vision of the darkness, I could see the glowing skeletons inching closer to me, their warped bones flashing in bright shades of blue, yellow, and green.

"Life support failure in three minutes. Return to *Titus-IV* immediately," the computer voice said calmly in my headset.

I had no way to get to the surface on my own. The creeping ghost skeletons encircled me. I counted eighteen of them, the same number as the crew of U-913. I called out one last time to my crewmates. The shimmering, transparent skeletons pointed their crooked, bony fingers at me like claws. The skeletons slowly opened and closed their jaws over and over, their teeth long and jagged, their eye-sockets glaring black pits. They stayed back, not moving any closer.

They watched me, waiting, as if they somehow knew that in only a few minutes I would join them forever.

Escape from Hell

KM Rockwood

Noise in the corridor outside my cell door startled me fully awake. Had I been sleeping? It was hard to tell. I spent most of the time in a dreamy half-awake state.

The murmuring voices grew softer. They came from the dark shadows back in the cell, a continual stream of chattering always a bit too low to make out any specific words. If there were specific words.

The tray slot in the cell door dropped open. Blinding light seared my eyes.

I blinked and grabbed the tray as it slid through. The slot started to close again.

"Hey." I licked my lips and tried to make my dry mouth form words. "Any news?"

The guard hesitated. "Maybe. They finished going through the videos of the riots. Made lists of IDs."

"And?"

"They're conducting individual disciplinary hearings. Go from there. Street charges, transfers to other prisons, stretches in disciplinary segregation. Stuff like that."

"How long is it gonna take until they get to me?"

"I dunno. They moved the ringleaders out right away. They're working on everybody else on the list."

"They won't show me doing anything." To tell the truth, I hadn't had much of a chance to do anything. Early on I got hit in the head with something, and spent most of the riot lying there unconscious.

"They're using other testimony, too," the guard said. "Inmates. Correctional officers. State police. Anybody who could have been involved."

"I just happened to be there. Didn't get involved at all. Suppose no one says anything about me joining in?" I hadn't done anything, and I didn't have any enemies that might testify against me for spite. At least that I knew of.

"If there's no evidence you participated, I guess you return to general population." He shut the slot with a definitive clang.

I stood in the semidarkness of the windowless cell, clutching the tray. The dank stone walls seemed to waver and close in. Over the years, most of the old prison had been upgraded. But not these old solitary confinement cells in the basement. The hole, they used to call it. I could see why. They weren't supposed to be in use anymore.

The muttering grew louder again. The voices sounded like they were arguing among themselves. I tried to ignore them.

The chilly air around me grew colder until icy fingers reached down under my shirt. I knew what that meant. The thing was absorbing energy in the form of heat from the air, and soon I would be able to see it.

A fluttering of leathery wings filled the air. An invisible weight landed on my shoulder. Claws dug in. A disembodied spectral finger poked at the tray in my hands. "What've we got?"

I closed my eyes and took a deep breath. "What'd ya think? Meal loaf. And it's *mine*, not *ours*."

The thing ignored that. "That stuff doesn't taste very good. Hardly qualifies as food."

I opened my eyes and watched as the indistinct gray mist perched on my shoulder took shape. Every time he moved, his features were more distinct, even in the uncertain light.

He looked like one of those gargoyles on the outsides of medieval cathedrals, hunched back, pointed horns and sharp teeth. His deep set eyes glowed.

This close, I could smell his damp foul breath.

I sighed. "The food's not supposed to be good. In segregation, all you get's meal loaf. It's all your food ground up together and baked in a loaf. You won't starve, but it tastes terrible."

"At least they feed you." The long pointed nail on the thing's finger speared a chunk off the slice of meal loaf and stuck it in his mouth. "And they give you a blanket. Lots of men have died down here. Just dumped and left. Starved. Or frozen. Not much difference." The thing grinned. "Once they're dead, I can't suck any more energy out of them. So I eat them."

"Well," I said. "They don't starve people to death any more. At least on purpose. And they don't much use these basement cells, either. But with the riot, they ran out of segregation cells. So here I am."

He poked at the tray. "It's been years since anybody's been locked up here long enough to see me."

"Lucky me."

He cocked his head. "You don't have to be sarcastic."

"I can be sarcastic if I want to. Especially since you're just a figment of my imagination."

"That's an insult. Not true."

I looked at the tray. The piece of meal loaf the thing had taken was missing. That wasn't my imagination. But I said, "Sure it is. Everybody knows enough solitary confinement makes people crazy."

"Are you crazy?"

"Here I am, arguing with an imaginary creature over a share of my food. Doesn't that sound crazy to you?"

"Not really. Except for the 'imaginary creature' part. Lots of the men who've ended up here have been *really* crazy."

"Maybe you're really a ghost of one of those men," I said.

"Nah. I'm no ghost. The ghosts just sit around and talk all the time. Don't you hear them?"

So that's what the chattering voices were. "Why don't they go on to the next world?"

The thing gave a cackling laugh. "Most of them don't want to."

"Why not?"

"'Cause they'll go straight to hell. You know what some of them have done?"

"No." I shivered. I didn't want to know.

"All kinds of stuff. Two of them killed their mothers. One beat his baby to death. And there's the one guy who likes to torture women. Grab them off the street and tie them up and cut them into little pieces."

"Why did he do that?"

"He says it's fun. Especially watching their eyes. He likes to duct tape their mouths shut and cut off bits. Ears. Fingers. Toes. Then he holds the pieces in front of their faces to show them."

"Well, at least once he got to prison, he couldn't get at any women anymore."

"True. But then he did it to his cell mate. Cut off his penis. And his balls, too. That's why they put the guy down here, by himself. He'd like to do it again."

A stab of fear cut through my gut. "Is he one of the voices I hear?"

"Yep."

"And he wants to tie me up and cut me into little pieces?"

"Sure. I mean, he doesn't want to do it to *you* specifically. But it's been years since anybody's been down here. He'd take whoever he could get."

Panic rose in my throat and I pushed the food tray aside. "Is he gonna try to do that?"

"Well, he can't. Not yet, anyhow. He needs to get a lot stronger before he's got enough physical presence to even be visible, much less do something like that." The thing speared another hunk of meal loaf. "Thanks. This may not be tasty, but I haven't had much to eat for a while now."

"But *you've* got a physical presence. Why doesn't he?"

"I've had more practice. I started working on it the first day you were down here. They thought you'd be moved in a day or two, so they didn't bother for a while. Besides, it's different for different kinds of creatures. I never died, so I never had to get together enough energy to come back from the dead. I'm not a ghost."

I didn't find much comfort in that news. "What, exactly, are you?"

"A demon. A very minor one." He leaned his head forward and reached his forked tongue into the cup of water on the tray.

"Where did you come from?"

"From hell, of course. That's where all demons come from."

"How'd you get here from hell?"

"Sometimes when enough evil gets concentrated in a small area, a tunnel opens up."

"Is that what happened here?" I asked.

"Yep. I managed to escape."

"Can't you get back?"

"I suppose I could. But I don't really want to. It's, you know, *hell* down there. If I can be someplace else, I'll take it."

"Even here, in this godforsaken cell?"

"Oh, yes. It's a lot better than hell. A hell of a lot better than hell." He snickered.

It wasn't comforting to know he was a demon, but at least I didn't have to call him the "thing" any more.

What was the matter with me? He wasn't real. My imagination had conjured him up. Along with the voices.

I rubbed a sore spot my head. During the riot, I'd taken a pretty solid blow to the head. Could be I had a concussion. Could be I was asleep and dreaming right now. Or hallucinating.

The guard came back to get the empty tray. The demon had eaten all the food and drank the water. I knew I'd be very hungry later, and sorry I'd let him have it all, but it was too late to worry about that now.

I lay down on the bunk and pulled the itchy blanket around me. It was damp and smelled musty, but it was made of wool and held some heat, even when it was wet.

The voices chattered on. They sounded more menacing than ever.

The demon settled himself onto the edge of the bunk, back in the corner.

What meal had that been? I'd lost track of time. I wished I'd started keeping track of the time by putting up a hash mark every time I got a meal.

Then I'd know that three were one day, and I'd have some idea of how long I'd been down here. For what good it would do.

And how much longer would I be here? For right now, I was being held on administrative segregation until my participation, or lack thereof, in the recent riots was investigated. Then I'd have a hearing. If found guilty, I'd probably be sent to a maximum security facility for a while. That wouldn't be much fun, but it would sure beat spending more time in this cell.

But I'd just been caught up in the crowd. Wrong place at the wrong time. When the announcement was made that all inmates not participating in the disturbance should return to their cell blocks, the one to which I was assigned was on fire. And then something'd hit me on the head.

By the book, they had ten days to hold the hearing. Given the circumstances and the number of hearings they'd need to hold, though, it wouldn't be surprising if they got an extension on that. And since they would tackle the obvious ringleaders first, followed by anyone they had good evidence on, mine might be one of the last hearings held.

The idea flitted across my mind that it might be worth it to tell the guard that I was ready to confess to participating in the riot to get out of here. It might even be worth it to claim I was a mastermind.

They'd think I was crazy, but that might not be far from the truth.

I closed my eyes, but I'd lost the ability to tell whether I was awake or asleep.

The demon hopped along the edge of the bunk, then climbed over me, his claws digging into my flesh. He lifted up a corner of the blanket and snuggled down under it, his cold scaly skin against my back. I shivered.

When had I started seeing him?

I startled alert to a banging on the cell door. The slot opened, letting in the blinding light. The demon hopped onto the floor and stretched his wings. Funny. He had always disappeared when there was more light. Was he getting stronger?

"Get up. Time for your hearing," a guard said.

At last. I stumbled over to the door.

"Put your hands through the slot."

I did so. I almost welcomed the cold steel of the handcuffs on my wrists. I could tell they were real.

The door swung open. The light hurt my eyes.

One guard held my elbow while the other slapped on leg irons and a waist chain.

His nose wrinkled. I probably stank. When was the last time I'd had a shower?

Propelled by the pressure on my elbow, I shuffled out into the corridor.

As they slammed the door shut, the gray shape of the demon shimmered through the opening and fluttered up to my shoulder.

How come I could see him here? And why was he outside the cell?

"What are you doing?" I asked him.

The guard looked at me, frowning. "Taking you for your disciplinary hearing."

The demon waited until he was finished talking and grinned at me. "No, of course they can't see me. Or hear me."

I shrugged my shoulder, trying to unseat him. "Get off me."

"Whoa, dude. Easy," one of the guards said, tightening his grip on my arm. "We're here to escort you to the hearing room. Just come along quietly."

The demon grinned at me. "I'm going with you."

I stood still. "Why the hell are you doing that?"

The guard shook his head. "They're processing everybody as quick as they can. Your number must have just come up. It'll go much better if you cooperate."

The demon hunched down on my shoulder, his claws holding firmly. "I need to get my energy from someone alive. It's been decades since anybody's been in that cell."

"You gonna *stay* with me?" I asked.

"Somebody will," the guard said.

"It might be decades before anyone is there again. I'm not going back," the demon said.

"Going back to hell?" I asked.

The guards looked at each other. "They're moving people on, regardless.

Even if you end up in segregation, it probably won't be that hellhole you've been in. But you got to go to the hearing."

The demon stretched his head over to my ear and nibbled on it. "You're my source of strength. We'll have a lot of fun together."

"No!" I swallowed a sob.

"Sorry, dude. You gotta go. We can do this the easy way, or the hard way. But you're gonna go."

They shoved me forward.

I stumbled. One of the guards caught me before I fell. He looked at his partner. "They shouldn't have opened up these old segregation cells," he said. "Looking for trouble if you ask me."

"Yeah. Lock anyone up in one long enough, alone, and he's gonna go crazy."

Buffalo Blonde

BG House

Jesse Dunker didn't really know why people laughed at him behind his back. He always caught the winks, but he figured he'd just missed out on a good joke.

A lanky young man born and bred in Buffalo Trail, Montana, he'd flunked the cop test after high school and gone to work for his father, Old Joe "Thumb Sucker" Dunker, who didn't outgrow the habit until he was in his teens. Old Joe owned the largest used car lot in the county. Jesse, who'd picked up his father's peculiar habit, would detail the cars, write the prices on the windshields, and check the doors to make sure they were locked. He even managed to sell a few, so he wasn't entirely worthless. His standard sales pitch was, "Hey, have I got the car that'll make you look like a million bucks."

One sultry afternoon, when he was leaning on the hood of a '99 Chevy Malibu, he saw a beautiful blonde across the street.

The blonde was flitting between the cars at Buffalo Chrysler Jeep Dodge, the new car lot and their biggest competitor. Sunlight caught her hourglass figure, bright yellow dress, gossamer shawl, and white shoes as a hapless salesman trailed her from car to car. She had to be a hippie or even a movie star, although what a movie star would be doing in Buffalo Trail was a mind-blowing mystery.

Jesse smiled across the street, pleased when the blonde flashed a smile back at him. She gave a little wave and began to cross the pavement. He straightened up from the Malibu and brushed off his jacket, feeling a funny lump in his throat.

"Excuse me, mister, you sell used cars?" she asked in a sweet voice.

"Yes ma'am, we do," Jesse managed to sputter. Everything about the woman was so blindingly golden yellow, from her honeyed hair to her yellow dress, that he almost felt intoxicated. Looking at her face was like gazing into the heart of a perfect yellow daffodil.

"Well, I have two thousand dollars and I need a car that can get me out to my home and back, reliable," she said, looking around at the dozens of cars and trucks.

Had to be a hippie. A movie star would've bought a new car. In fact, a movie star wouldn't have even bothered to cross the street.

"Have I got a car that'll make you look like a million bucks," Jesse said, grinning.

"Don't you think I already look like a million?" she cooed.

"A million and change," Jesse found himself saying to the woman, a drop of drool escaping from the corner of his mouth.

"Can you show me around then?"

He set out across the car lot with the gorgeous blonde at his side.

"We got a 2001 Hyundai Santa Fe with only 60,000 on her," he said. "Rides like a dream and gets around real good in the winter."

She gave him another spellbinding smile. "How about something smaller?"

"I got a yellow '67 VW Beetle that might be up your alley. It's got a couple of dents, but we can pull them out."

"Yellow, my favorite color," she murmured, tucking a strand of golden hair behind her ear.

"You want to test drive it around town?"

Another smile. "Sure thing. Just give me the keys."

"Ma'am, I have to go with you." Even though Jesse was famously slow on the uptake, his father had drummed that one into him.

They came to the bright yellow Beetle. As soon as Jesse opened the door, the blonde slid into the driver's seat. Jesse tried to sit in the back so he wouldn't make her nervous, but he couldn't bend his tall frame into the cramped quarters. Running around to the front, he managed to squeeze in the passenger seat with his knees pressed up against his chest.

The blonde put her foot on the accelerator and off they went, shooting down the boulevard to Main Street, gaining speed as they passed the grocery, the Exxon, and the library. Seconds later, she flew off Main onto Crooked Creek Road, taking the curves at such high speeds that Jesse had to grip the seat to keep from flying into the windshield.

"Ma'am, I have to ask you to slow it down," he gasped.

She laughed. "If I slow down, how'll I know if it can take what I dish out?"

Jesse had no answer for that question. Shooting him another smile, the blonde sped through the wide open countryside and across the creek until she reached a wooded crest, where she abruptly hit the brakes. Jesse flew forward and smashed his chin on his knees, letting out a yowl.

"Now what?" he said, rubbing his face and inspecting his palm for blood.

"I'm here. Thanks for the ride. I'll be back to town in a couple of days and maybe I'll buy this ol' thing from you."

Slipping out of the car, she raced in her white shoes up the hill. Dumbfounded, Jesse slowly stepped out into the hot sunlight. He strained his neck trying to follow her yellow dress and gossamer shawl as she ran into the trees, but he soon lost sight of the beautiful blonde completely. A hippie for sure. He craned his neck again. She had to be living out there in some little place he couldn't quite see.

***

Back at the lot, Jesse closed up for the day. He got into the 1977 Pinto Runabout his father had sold him and drove off to see his mother. She was recovering from a stroke at Happy Endings Nursing Home.

Visiting Happy Endings was always a mixed blessing. He walked down the main corridor, wading through the bent-over wheelchair people who looked like melted wax stuck in their chairs. Some of the old men and women reached out to grab his hands, asking for help, whispering, even begging him to save them from shadowy fears that only they could see.

Finally, just when he couldn't bear the sadness of the place, he arrived at Room 127. There Mrs. Betsy Dunker sat crocheting a wool beanie for him, even though it was summer. After they greeted each other and he asked what she'd had for dinner (chicken, mashed potatoes, and peach pie), she wanted to know about his day at the lot.

"Well, Ma, I might've sold that old Beetle to a woman who lives outside town."

"What's her name?" his mother asked.

He shook his head. "I don't know."

She pursed her lips. "Then how do you know you're going to sell her a car? You know, Jesse, I love you dearly, but you've never been the tallest corn in the row."

"Now, Ma, don't start. She said she was coming back to buy it."

"And how many times have people fed you that line?"

"Ma, I'm going now. Love you."

Jesse kissed his mother on the forehead and headed back through the wheelchair people to the front lawn, relieved to find himself in the sunlight again. His mother was right. How did he know the blonde would come back? And how would the blonde get back into town when she didn't have a car? But, man, she sure was pretty. The memory of her golden hair and sunny yellow dress intoxicated him all over again.

***

The next day, Jesse shaved, chose his best clothes, and prepped to go out to the blonde's house to offer to bring her into town to buy the car. He even remembered the hill where they'd stopped. Her place couldn't be too far from there. Cramming himself into the yellow Beetle, he drove out of town at a reasonable speed this time until he reached the summit of the hill where the blonde had taken off.

Standing there, he looked around 360 degrees. No house, barn, farm, or anything, just a stand of trees and a pile of sundried logs. But he was almost positive it was the place.

"Now think!" he told himself angrily. "Don't go mixing stuff up. You have to remember." He placed his favored thumb up to his mouth and then caught himself and stopped.

Just as he was getting back into the Beetle, he was stunned to see the blonde in the passenger seat, wearing a blue dress this time with tiny yellow flowers. She'd crossed her shapely legs, showing off her matching yellow shoes. Her flaxen hair was tied in a golden bow and her skin glowed like cream, like she'd stepped out of some crazy fairy tale.

Jesse stared. "Now how'd the heck you get in here?"

She smiled. "Just got right on in."

"From where?" He looked around in confusion.

"Over yonder," she said, pointing over her shoulder into the nothingness of the vast Montana countryside.

None of it made any sense. Dumbstruck by her beauty, Jesse said, "I thought you might want to buy the car today."

"I might. I do need to go to town."

He didn't know quite what to do next except start up the car and head to town.

"So you really think you might buy the car?" he repeated.

"After I go to the bank and get the money, I might."

"So you want to go to the bank?"

"Not yet, I want to go to Abeja Salon. Do you like my hair?"

"Yes, ma'am," he said, staring at her golden waves. "You got the most beautiful hair I've ever seen. I've never seen anybody with hair like yours."

Jesse dropped off the blonde at the salon. Just as she was leaving the car, he called, "Hey, what's your name?" but she either didn't hear him or just ignored him. Returning to the lot, he was no closer to the sale or knowing who she was than when he'd started out.

At lunchtime, he wandered down to the local diner where he ate every day. He ordered the meatloaf special, pie, and coffee.

"Apple or pecan today?" Maureen, the sour-faced server, asked him.

"Apple. Say, have you seen that hot blonde around, looking for a car? Lives outside of town."

"Not me, no hot blondes here. Ask Willis. He always snoops around in everybody's business."

"Thanks, Maureen." Jesse left a small tip and moved to the back of the diner where Willis, the fat sheriff, was shoving a sandwich in his mouth.

"Sheriff, how you doing," Jesse began.

"Fine until now," the sheriff said with his mouth full of food. "Whadda you want? I got five minutes to eat my lunch."

Probably on his second lunch by now, Jesse thought. "I was wondering if you've seen a blonde around today."

"What'd she do? Steal one of your cars?"

"Oh, no, no, she wants a buy a car. A real hot blonde."

"Jesse, if I came across a real hot blonde, why on earth would I tell you of all people? Maybe you mean Nancy at the Exxon. When she takes her cap off, I think her hair is sorta blonde."

"Sorta gray," Maureen corrected.

"I'm looking for a blonde." A little embarrassed, Jesse stared at his shoes.

He took off for the hair salon to see if he would run into the blonde, but the modern, brightly lit salon turned out to be mostly empty of customers. A twentyish woman with black painted fingernails who was texting on her Smartphone reluctantly looked up.

Jesse leaned on the counter. "Kris, I dropped off a blonde this morning. Have you seen her? She's real pretty."

She smirked. "Now Jesse, you know I don't curl and tell."

"Come on, it's important. She might buy a car."

"A blonde came in this morning but she didn't say much. I wouldn't call her pretty, though." Coming from Kris, that was no guarantee of anything. Kris's idea of pretty was Morticia from the Addams Family. "She paid cash. She didn't leave her name or anything."

He rubbed his hand over his jaw. "Man, she's hard to track down."

"Good luck selling that car."

***

Right around five o'clock, Jesse sat down in the office, feet up on the desk, to Google the MLB sports scores. The computer crashed. The thing had to be a million years old and his father was too cheap to buy a new one. Annoyed, Jesse picked up a copy of Used Car Weekly with a Buick LaSalle centerfold that the old man had been reading. Glancing up, he was shocked to see the blonde standing there with her hair curling over her shoulders. She was the picture of golden gorgeousness.

Jesse leaped out of his chair. "Sorry, I didn't hear you come in."

She smiled at him. "I never had time to get to the bank, but I thought maybe you'd give me a ride home."

"Absolutely, ma'am," Jesse said.

As they passed out of town, he drove with care, paying attention to every single turn that she asked him to make. This time he was going to nail down the way to her house.

"Thanks for the ride," the blonde said, opening the car door.

"It's Jesse. Jesse Dunker. But you can call me Jess."

"Okay, Jess, see you later."

"What about the car?"

"I'll be back in touch, Jess."

"Can I walk you to your door?"

Before he could finish the sentence, the blonde was over and down the hill. Jesse leaped out of the car and peered down in the direction she had gone. There seemed to be absolutely no trace of her.

Mystified beyond anything he'd ever felt in his life, he sat in the car, thinking about the strange situation until the sun finally set. Twilight spread over the hill, casting odd shadows. The stars came out in full brilliance. He'd always felt at home in the big sky country, but that night the spookiness of the open land began to get under his skin. Tired and hungry, he finally started the car and headed home, looking through the rear view mirror. Not a single house or farm and no sight of the blonde.

***

Saturday rolled around, the busiest day of the week on the lot. Bobby Jeffries always showed up to work the weekend. An older, experienced salesman, he sported a full head of silver hair, weathered skin, and a smile as wide as the Missouri River. And he always sold cars, sometimes as few as one, but usually more than that.

Jesse found Saturdays the hardest days to work, knowing he would be outdone. That Saturday he ended the day without selling a single car.

Shrugging off his disappointment, he chugged home in the old Pinto, popped open a Bud, and turned on the Big Sky Little League game. Right at the second inning, he began to think about the blonde in the yellow dress and wondered if she really was going to buy the car from him. He couldn't do anything until Monday. Nobody in town moved a finger on Sunday except to haul themselves off to church.

Restless, Jesse flipped off the game and headed to the used car lot. Bobby Jeffries had dimmed the lights in the showroom and locked up. No one else was around, so he got the key to the Beetle and cruised out of town.

"I should ask her out," he told himself. "She could be mine."

Summer air rich with fragrant honeysuckle and clover blew through the Beetle's open window. The sun hadn't even set yet. There was plenty of time to do anything they wanted. He felt a tingle of excitement as he neared the last place he'd seen the blonde. Maybe she'd even go to the movies with him.

Just as he crested the hill, a bee flew in the open window and stung him in the eye.

"Hey," he shouted, waving the bee away from his face. The bee was still in the car. He could see it crawling inside the windshield.

When he tried to swat it with his hand, the car swerved, but he managed to keep the tires on the road. Out of nowhere, another bee stung his bottom lip. He tried to swat it away, too. The damn things had to be swarming. How did he drive into a swarm of bees?

To his horror, his eye was swelling shut. His other eye was watering so badly it was like looking though a fishbowl. Once again, a bee dive-bombed, stinging him on his temple. His vision grew so milky that tears rolled down his cheeks. More bees crawled across the steering wheel, stinging his fingers and the back of his hands. They flew down his shirt and stung the top of his head and ears.

"Get outta here," he screamed, waving his hands while he struggled to control the car.

Seconds later, he lost sight of where he was going. The car careened down the hill, hit the old pile of logs, and flipped over with a terrible thud. Jesse smashed his head on the dashboard and lay there, dazed. He was vaguely aware that the horn was blasting, but he couldn't move his arms to stop it. Thousands of bees rose in a black cloud from the logs by the car window. They swirled inside the car, buzzing and stinging him through his clothes. In the middle of the nightmarish noise he heard a familiar voice.

"I'm zorry, Jezzzzze."

In agony, he cracked his paralyzed eye and the milky good one and saw the blonde without any clothes on, her tiny wings flapping rapidly as she hovered over the dashboard.

Was it really her? How did she get to be so small?

"I wanted you to be mine," he slurred.

"No, you're the one whooozzz mine now," she buzzed.

The massive hive swarmed into every inch of the Beetle. Bees crawled over the stick shift and the AM/FM radio knobs and squeezed their black and yellow bodies into the air-conditioning vents. He could barely breathe. Hundreds of bees stung his nose and cheeks and mouth. His sight faded.

Then something smooth and warm dripped across his skin. Wax, he realized with dull incredulity. It grew harder to take a breath as his swelling throat closed up. Buzzing filled his ears as his senses dimmed, but just before he lost consciousness he realized the bees were pushing and pulling the wax into a hexagon shape as they encased him in the car. *Royyyal jelly*, they buzzed in a chorus into his swollen ears. *Royal jelly for the queeeen.*

The Secret Life of Sam Dunlap

BG House

Mrs. Baxter placed the cold rib-eye steak in the searing hot iron skillet. The meat sizzled the second it hit the pan.

"Over easy, black and blue," ninety-one-year-old Sam Dunlap hollered.

"I know, I know, bloody rare. I've been cooking the same breakfast for you forever," she called from the kitchen. "You sure were up late last night. I'll have to start keeping the lights on for you."

It was 6:35 a.m. and Sam performed his ortho-recommended stretches while lying in his overstuffed bed. The coffee Mrs. Baxter was making wafted the aroma of freshly crushed beans through the house. His nose delighted in the sweet smell of frying flesh as he limped down the hall to the kitchen.

The ageless Mrs. Baxter turned the giant steak with a long, thin fork. She had worked for Sam as a live-in for fifty years, but she still had beautiful blue-black hair that she coiled into a tight bun on the back of her head. Never a strand misplaced. Always dressed in a white silk blouse and black pencil skirt. Sam found himself staring at her lithe body until she turned and glared at him with her piercing green eyes.

"Is it ready yet?" Sam asked, literally drooling now.

"If you don't start eating more carbs, you'll waste away, and you know what Doc Sanders says about that, don't you?"

"All right, I'll eat a damn biscuit," he said, pretending to eat it by pulling it apart with his arthritic fingers, spreading it across the plate. Mrs. Baxter looked down at the small round plate with the scattered biscuit leavings and shook her head. Sam's eyes met hers with an expression of total innocence.

***

Sam opened the newspaper to the front page. Another gruesome murder in the Truman Park last night. Victim literally torn apart. No suspects as of yet. The police were questioning everyone. He stared at the headline as a large lump grew in his throat. How awful, he thought.

Picking up the Old Farmer's Almanac, he checked the weather, the sunrise and sunset, and the moon phases as he did every morning. As he read on, he sucked in and out, rubbing his tongue along his few yellowed teeth, noticing that one was loose. He played with it with his sticky, dry tongue, then downed the last of his coffee and glanced at the clock. By this time, he had finished his nearly raw steak, cleaning the plate up with another leftover biscuit.

Time for his morning neighborhood watch. Sam grabbed his walker, pulled himself up, and clomped into the living room to his well-worn rocking chair. Swinging his body around, he placed his scrawny rear in the chair with a *whomp*, almost knocking the breath out of himself. As he settled down, he placed an orange hand-knit blanket across his legs. Once he'd seated himself, he could survey everything that went on in the front yard, the neighbor's yard, and some of the side yards. But soon, he was fast asleep.

He woke up with a start. A commotion of barking, snarling and growling ripped through the air. It was the Wilson dog Proton, threatening the very life of the mail carrier.

"Shut up, you stupid, mangy mutt," Sam rasped. He hated to hear that dog go on and on. From the look of his jaws, Proton would truly be a menace to the neighborhood if he ever got loose. Sam didn't much like the Wilsons themselves, either. Rob Wilson was the vice president of Tri-City Bank and his wife Elsa an uppity-up nurse at the county hospital. Their four children ran around like banshees in Sam's yard. They were just another huge annoyance. All he wanted was peace and quiet in his senior years.

***

Later on, Mrs. Baxter announced that she was going out for the afternoon since Sunday was sort of her day off. She made Sam a ham and cheese sandwich and got him a bottle of beer, the same lunch he had eaten for the last twenty years.

"I'll be back to make your dinner, Mr. Dunlap," Mrs. Baxter called as she put on her coat and scarf.

"No need for dinner tonight, Mrs. Baxter, my gout's acting up and I think I'll just have a can of soup," he called back as she shut the door.

Sam didn't have much of an appetite after all, decided to skip the soup, and headed to bed early. He dragged the walker down the hall to his bedroom. There, he locked his bedroom door. Never can be too careful, he thought, remembering the murder in the paper. Yawning, he took his robe off, climbed back into bed, and began to read the third Harry Potter book. He really loved Hagrid.

Time passed quickly as he poured over the story. He read and dozed for hours. Finally, he closed the book and placed it on the nightstand, took off his glasses, and rubbed his weak, watery blue eyes. Looking up, he saw a magnificent full moon shining directly through the sheer curtains.

In spite of feeling beat, Sam crawled out from under the covers and threw his spindly legs over the edge of the bed. He felt a rumbling from within and a whimper come out of his mouth. His skinny arms and legs transmuted from geriatric limbs to the sinewy fore and hind legs of a very large animal. Long, yellow, cracked nails appeared on his arthritic paws. He fell onto the floor, painfully rolling back and forth as his body continued to morph into doglike features.

His skin went from papery thin to a hide of clumpy, irregular, silvery skin and fur. His ribs stuck out like piano keys and his tail came out crooked and bald. His snout grew by inches and his fangs mimicked his old man teeth, worn to nibs with his best teeth missing altogether. As he licked his chops with his parched tongue, out popped the loose tooth, only now it was a front fang.

Blinking his pale, moist eyes, he turned and saw himself in the full length mirror, finally understanding what had happened. He could smell decay on his breath. Groaning with agony, he stood up on all fours. Every joint in his body ached as if it needed oiling.

"Woof!" he managed instead of a real wolf's cry. How pathetic he had become. Sam, the great and mighty, was now a sack of bones and tufts of hair on quivering legs with a crooked tail.

But the moon was full and it was his time. He tried to leap out the window, but his scrawny legs couldn't lift up his body. So, with his front paws hanging out, he let gravity do the rest, ending up in a crumpled pile on the holly bush outside. He shook himself ever so slightly, hoping not to break something, and wobbled out into the bright moonlight.

"Hey, look who's still here, what's-his-werewolf," a large juvenile wolf barked.

"I think we'll call him Sam the Weak and Wimpy," another said.

"Hey there, Sam, ignore the pups. You ready for the kill tonight, old boy," the senior said, circling around Sam, sniffing him up and down. Sam could feel the wolf's warm breath on his hind legs.

"Hello, Rob, Elsa, pups. Glad to see you out on such a fine night," Sam said with a congested huff. He really did hate the Wilsons. "Don't think I'll be able to keep up tonight, getting a little slow, you know."

Soon everyone stood still with the fur on their backs bristling upward. All snouts tipped in the air at once, smelling an unsuspecting visitor. A poor, misguided brown rabbit had hopped right into the midst of the werewolf welcome wagon.

"There ya go, old Sam, he's frozen in place just for you. Surely you can take *him* out," Rob said, egging Sam on.

Sam snorted and groped the ground. As he inhaled deeply, he leaped at the rabbit, only to hit the hard ground. The Wilson pack howled with laughter as the rabbit hopped on into the thicket.

Sam slowly picked himself up from the ground with a low growl.

"I think I'll do better hunting on my own," he said to the werepack, licking his left paw. "I'll be fine."

Sam started to turn from them but noticed they were, in fact, surrounding him. Their fangs out, sopping wet with drool. Rob's red eyes stared into Sam's like fire.

"Um, guess I'll be on my way," Sam said, as he lowered his head almost to the ground, showing submission.

"And you'll be going where?" Rob growled.

"Thought I might just stay in the neighborhood and see if there are any vermin to be had," Sam sputtered. "I won't be in your way at all."

"Or maybe we should just put you out of your fermenting, old, disgusting misery right now. What'd ya think, y'all?" Rob bayed as he dug into the frozen grass and snarled.

Being outnumbered and outmuscled, Sam could only look back up at the moon and long for his end to finally happen, but not this way. Not by his own. Not here and not now.

"You know, Rob, if you start to chew on me, all you'll get is wiry fur and sinew. You might even get a nasty little case of parvo," Sam said desperately but convincingly, licking his lips and panting.

"Parvo?" Rob woofed. "Elsa, is that true?"

"Could be, Robbie, so I don't want near him," Elsa whined. "Parvo can kill. Let's let him go. He'll just freeze to death by morning."

The pack bayed again with glee, strutting off across the street into the bushes. Sam sat there feeling as though he had been that little rabbit. The frost on the ground was making his butt shiver, so he stood up and walked down the dimly lit sidewalk toward the park. If there were critters to be had, the park was the place. As he took a step toward the park, his ears pricked up. Footfalls crunched on the grass behind him. Panicking, Sam hobbled as fast as he could down an alley and through an unlatched gate. A backyard. The moon shone brightly into the yard except for the very corners by the fence. Sam looked around one way, then the other, and then heard a chilling sound, a guttural, lip-licking snuffle of hoarse breathing.

Proton, the Wilson Rottweiler-Mastiff mix.

"Hey, Proton, it's me, Sam, nice night, huh?" Sam said timidly.

Proton peered through the shadows of the garbage cans, breathing so heavily that he snorted puffs of steam from his nostrils. Sam slowly stepped back, keeping his eyes on the dog while he tried to figure out how to get out of there. Suddenly, Proton sprang forward, a trail of saliva flowing in the air behind him. He landed right on top of Sam, his breath smelling of cheap dog food as he pinned the old werewolf to the ground.

"So, what in the hell are you doing in MY yard, you pathetic wolf-thing?" Proton barked. His white fangs gleamed in the moonlight. "You must have a death wish, Dunlap."

"Proton, really, I didn't know it was your yard," Sam stuttered, trying to wiggle loose.

"You chump, I've been waiting for a chance to snag you in the alley and take a huge bite out of your wimpy, decrepit body. Now you're here and I have you on my home turf," Proton slobbered, watching the fear in Sam's widening eyes.

"But, but, Proton, I'm not worth it, I have parvo," Sam confessed.

"Parvo, who cares, I go to the best vets in town. I'm a Wilson after all!" the dog snorted.

"Yeah? And you're just a mangy D-O-G," Sam said, spitting out the letters.

How could the great Sam Dunlap be pinned by this lesser breed? Mustering up all his strength, Sam writhed and arched until he threw Proton to the ground. Surprising even himself, he stood there, panting with a vicious grin that showed what was left of his crooked yellow teeth. His eyes squinted into a staredown with Proton. Neither moved an inch. Finally, they orbited one another in an ancient death dance. Only one of them was leaving the yard alive.

Sam's heart beat wildly in his chest. His hind legs trembled and his stomach churned, but he remained steady. Lightheaded, he felt the yard swim around him like a spinning wheel. Not now. Sam forced himself to stand. *Don't keel over now.* That would be too easy. His head throbbed. His mouth went dry. He tried to draw a deep breath but sharp pains stabbed his ribs. He looked at the gate. It seemed miles away. If he could just get through the gate, it would latch behind him and he would be free.

But Sam began to weaken again, panting as they danced.

"Looks like you're a wasted werewolf, Sam-my," barked Proton cruelly as he stopped circling and moved in for the kill.

Sam backed up with each step that Proton made toward him. Soon, he felt his rear up against the tree that Proton's people tied the dog all day. He could smell Proton's shit everywhere. He could see into his fierce eyes. Sam slowly moved around the tree, stumbling on the big, outstretched roots. He had nowhere to go. He had to stay and fight.

Shadows created by the moonlight hid Sam from sight against the tree. Proton stepped forward, roaring with anger.

Seizing the moment, Sam charged for Proton's neck, piercing the shorthaired skin with his stubby incisors. Proton yowled. Sam held on to his neck as he whipped back and forth, trying to free himself. Sam's jaw ached as he clenched down harder and harder. Sour blood poured into his mouth.

But sadly, Sam could hold on no longer. His old teeth gave way. The next buck of Proton's body ripped Sam's teeth out of his snout, leaving him with bleeding, dripping gums and his stubby teeth wedged in the monstrous dog's neck.

Once Proton realized he was free, he reared up on his hind legs, striking Sam with his sharp claws, his jaws wide open for the final assault. He tore into Sam like a T-bone.

When the old werewolf felt the sheer power of the dog slam into his forehead, he reared up, but his eyes filled with blood. The dog opened his gaping mouth and ripped off a huge piece of Sam's thigh. Howling in agony, Sam tried to hide behind the one tree in the yard, but Proton was after more blood.

Then Proton's howl changed to a high whine and yelp. His next lunge missed Sam.

Turning his head to see what was happening, Sam saw a flash of black and heard a loud hiss and spit. Moonlight shone on razorlike talons.

"Meeeeeooooow," the black cat called to Sam as it rode Proton's back. Still mewing, the cat climbed up Proton's back. The dog turned his head to attack, but the cat slashed his nose so badly that it almost fell off. Blood gushed everywhere. Howling, Proton rolled over on his back, paws up around his mangled nose as the cat disappeared over the fence.

Sam limped to the gate and pushed it open with his head. When he looked back, Proton lay on the ground, whimpering. There was no sign of the cat. The gate closed and latched behind the old werewolf as he made his way home, leaving a bloody trail of saliva on the ground.

***

Light shone brightly through the crack in the front door. Sam crept up the steps, sniffed the air inside, and pressed the door open just wide enough for his bony body to get through. The warm house felt good to his old, cold carcass. He stayed on the runner to keep his claws from clicking on the bare floor. Gathering up his strength, he crept to his room and pushed the door with his head. It didn't budge.

Then Sam remembered he had locked the door from the inside just before he fell out the window on the holly bush. Damn. So, he shuffled back down the hall to the kitchen.

Mrs. Baxter stood there, meticulously washing her hands at the sink, humming a little tune. She stopped to look up and stare into space.

"You really have been making trouble in the neighborhood, I see," she said. "I suppose you have an explanation for yourself."

Sam merely whimpered and sighed and opened his mouth in a way to show her he was now toothless. Turning around, Mrs. Baxter looked into his bloody mouth and weary eyes.

"I am afraid we're too old for this. You and I have been doing this for too many years to count," she said sympathetically. "Let's see, I have some freshly ground sirloin and some beer."

He looked at her longingly, nodding his gray head. She put a plate of beef and a bowl of beer on the floor for him as she placed a second plate of beef and a saucer of milk on the table for herself. He noticed that she slightly favored one leg as she walked.

"It's been a long night, Mr. Dunlap."

Sam gummed his hamburger and lapped up his beer. Afterwards, he walked up to Mrs. Baxter and licked her hand ever so gently.

The sun would be up in a few minutes. It had been a long night indeed.

The Bad Thing

HA Grant

The Bad Thing happened the summer I turned ten years old. It stayed with me all the years that followed, haunting the dark corners of my mind. We think we know reality, the same yellow sun that rises every day, the same stars that shine at night, until the moment it all slips sideways into the unthinkable.

It began with a simple splinter that infected my mother's hand. The doctor prescribed antibiotics. That night my mother broke out in oozing blisters. She'd always had a problem with medicine and had to wear a bracelet because she couldn't take penicillin. Soon she grew too weak to do anything except lie on the couch. Since my father was in Iraq, my mother and I went to stay with my aunt and uncle so they could take care of her. Somehow she managed to drive to their house in the Pennsylvania countryside by pulling over to rest on the side of the road every twenty minutes. I wasn't sure we were going to make it, but we finally did.

A knot grew in my stomach when we rolled up the driveway. Uncle David opened the car door to take our suitcases with his calloused hands. Aunt Agnes hurried behind him, frowning and tucking a wisp of hair back in her bun.

But the real joy waited on the porch. My thirteen-year-old cousin Janey lingered there with a sly smirk. Janey the Bully. Everything about her was the same. The straight blonde hair that made her look like an angel until she opened her mean mouth, the tough hands that had punched me in the stomach the last trip, the fakey-nice pink shorts she wore over her tanned sausage legs.

Two steps up the porch and my feet tangled up with something hard that shot out of nowhere. Janey's shoe. I hit the steps and landed hard on the sidewalk.

Hey, Frizz," Janey said under her breath. That was a crack about my unruly brown hair.

She had braces this year. If I'd been a sharper kid I would've called her Circuit Board or Metal Mouth, but I was a mouse and she knew it.

My aunt and uncle were still helping my mother out of the car. They'd turned their backs to the porch. They didn't notice my fall, but my mother's head shot up.

"Margaret?" she called in alarm.

"She just tripped. I'll help her," Janey said innocently.

Too terrified to look at my cousin, I scrambled up, breathing hard. The adults were behind us now. It felt like entering prison with every step into the house. Sharing a bedroom with Janey was going to be the worst. My aunt clomped up the stairs behind me to show me where to put my things. "Here's your bed," she said, pointing to the twin bed by Janey's under the dormer windows. "You and Janey will have so much fun together." In your dreams. Adults could be so clueless. I made sure the lock was on my suitcase and fled downstairs before Janey could trap me up there. How was I going to sleep in the same room with her?

My mother took the guest room on the first floor so she wouldn't have to climb upstairs. Which was good for her, but she wouldn't be upstairs to protect me.

"I want you to help out while you're here," she said weakly, lying back on the soft white pillows. The drive had really worn her out. "We need to be good guests. Aunt Agnes is going to give you a chore."

"You're going to weed and water the garden, Margaret," Aunt Agnes told me, taking me out to the vegetable garden behind the house. She wiped her hands on her apron. "Not today, though. In the morning when it's cooler."

Weeding was a perfect excuse to get out of the house and away from Janey. In spite of my aunt's instructions, I got down on my hands and knees and started pulling up weeds right then and there. Anything to keep from going inside again.

But fifteen minutes later I was burning up from the heat. Sweat drenched my shirt and trickled down my face. I looked around for shade. The largest trees stood near the house, but I wanted to stay away from there. Beyond the garden, a mysterious, shady hillside sloped down toward the wild fields. Covered with ancient lilac bushes, the hillside's twisting labyrinth seemed to beckon me with its deep shade. By now I was desperate to cool off, so I crawled under those limbs into an amazing green world.

The huge lilacs could have been a thousand years old. I crept farther into the green gloom, carefully holding onto the crooked trunks to keep from slipping down the hillside. Gray roots jutted like wide shoulder blades out of the eroded ground, connected to more old roots that resembled arms and elbows belonging to some gigantic prehistoric creature that slumbered half-buried under the earth. Exploring that deep green world, I finally found a hollow in the bony roots where I could curl up.

Safe. Protected. Hidden. I'd found my secret sanctuary. If Janey tried to torture me, I could flee here. In my heart I knew she'd never explored this place.

The thick leaves drooped in the heat. I stroked the ancient knobby trunk that hid me.

"You need water," I whispered. "I'm going to water you tomorrow when I water the garden."

***

Aunt Agnes passed the potato salad. We were all sitting around the big oak table, even my mother, who'd crept out of her room after several hours of rest.

"Janey has her piano lesson tomorrow morning," my aunt told my mother. "I hope the music won't disturb you."

A smug smile spread over Janey's face.

"Oh, no, not at all," my mother answered. She was too polite to say anything else.

My aunt studied Janey's hands. "Look at those fingers. Born to be a classical pianist. Or a surgeon."

Uncle David rubbed Janey's head. "Our little genius. Tell them why you're practicing, little pigeon."

Sickening. I stared at the potatoes on my plate, trying to keep my mouth shut.

"Tryouts for Music Star," Janey burbled. "We're driving to Washington, D.C. next month." She swelled up under the beaming faces of her parents.

My mother managed a frozen smile. "Margaret earned two Girl Scout Cadette badges this year. Trailblazing and Babysitting."

Silence. Silverware clinked against the plates.

I wanted to die. My face burned with embarrassment. There was no way my pathetic Girl Scout badges could compete with the glamorous Music Star. Of course, Janey focused her smirking eyes on me all through dinner. I hung out in the living room as long as I could, watching TV. But finally my aunt clapped her hands and told us to go to bed.

Lying upstairs in the dark, I gripped the sheet, too scared to sleep. Janey was awake, but I couldn't make out her face. Still fighting sleep, I was so exhausted my eyes finally closed. Then I had a horrible dream that Janey was leaning over me.

My eyes snapped open. The dream was real. She was standing only a foot away with a pair of red handled scissors. Grinning at me with those metal teeth. Then she put the scissors down without explanation and picked up a hairbrush.

"Just brushing my hair, Frizz," she said. "My long, straight, beautiful hair, which you're going to see on TV soon. Don't you wish you were going to the tryouts? Too bad they don't have a category for losers. They wouldn't let you in anyway because you're ugly. Pot bottom ugly."

Twice as humiliated as before, I shrank under the sheets.

Morning came. Janey lay in her bed like a lump with her face to the wall. Watching my sleeping enemy with terror, I crept out of bed, dressed as quietly as I could, and slipped downstairs. Everybody else was still asleep.

Dew still covered the grass. I weeded for a few minutes and then pulled out the hose and began to water the garden. But the wild lilacs on the hill drew me closer again. Their leaves still drooped down.

"I'm going to water you, too," I whispered. "Just like I promised."

I dragged the hose through the wet grass as far as I could and began to spray the parched hillside. Water poured between the huge, bony roots and vanished into the dry earth as if the prehistoric creature slumbering under the ground in my imagination had been dying of thirst and was greedily slurping it all up. *More more* the roots seemed to groan. *Thirsty thirsty, water water, more more.* Grateful. I could feel their satisfaction in my own bones. Hauling the long green hose behind me, I moved along the hill and glanced back at the house.

Janey was watching me from the bedroom window.

***

"We don't water the lilacs. It's wasting water." Aunt Agnes frowned at me. She was standing in the kitchen, cooking breakfast.

So Janey had ratted on me.

"They needed water," I said timidly.

"Those wild lilacs have been there forever. They can fend for themselves. Don't water them again. It's just wasting water. You girls set the table."

My face burned with embarrassment again. Janey kept staring at me with that smug look. We all sat down together except for my mother, who'd stayed in bed.

My aunt's eyes narrowed. "Margaret, what did you do to your hair?"

I froze. "What do you mean?"

"Did you cut your hair? There's a big nasty chunk missing in the front."

Stunned, I felt across my forehead. My fingers found the missing chunk, cut down to my scalp. Half my bangs were gone. My eyes jumped to Janey's poker face. That's why she'd been standing over me in the dark. That's why she'd been holding the red scissors. She'd ruined my hair.

"I didn't cut my hair," I burst out. "Janey did it!"

"She did not," my uncle said angrily.

"She did so!" I blurted even louder. "She cut my hair! She did it when I was asleep!"

"Janey would never do that," my uncle said.

"She hates me and she's always trying to push me around and she tripped me on the porch yesterday on purpose—"

"That's enough," Aunt Agnes said coldly. "You're making that up. Apologize."

"No, I won't!" I jumped up. "I want my mother!"

"Your mother is sick. Don't you dare disturb her. Keep your voice down and go to your room. And you can stay up there until you tell Janey you're sorry."

***

Banished. Lying upstairs on my bed, I listened to the sounds of the house. A car crunched over the gravel driveway. Then the front door opened. Voices, an adult I didn't recognize. Footsteps. Quiet, then piano music rose through the floor. Plonk plonk a donk donk. Janey practicing to be a big star.

It was all so unfair. I wanted to go downstairs and fling myself on my mother's bed, but she'd closed her door and my aunt had given me such a severe look that I didn't dare try it.

I crept over to the mirror. My rotten cousin had chopped off half my bangs. They'd take weeks to grow back. How could they think I'd do that to myself? Were they that blind to their own monster of a kid?

I'd look like a freak all summer. Hot tears of anger welled up in my eyes.

"Not fair," I said to the walls. I knew what my mother would do once she saw my bangs. Haul me off for a pixie cut. I'd end up looking like a boy. Or like I was seven years old.

My hair looked *awful.*

Eventually, the music stopped. More sounds came up through the floor. People walking around downstairs. Doors opening and closing.

It felt like I'd been lying upstairs in that prisonlike room for hours.

Then I heard my mother's voice at the front door. Worried, I hurried to the window and saw my uncle guide my mother into his red truck. She slumped next to him in the passenger seat with her head against the window. Janey and my aunt followed him. My aunt said something to Janey with a worried furrow between her eyes and slipped in beside my mother.

My heart leaped. Where were they taking her? To a store? She wasn't strong enough to walk around. They'd forgotten all about me. That realization really hurt. Gripping the windowsill, I watched the truck disappear down the road.

Janey turned back toward the house with her eyes on the bedroom window. I moved behind the curtains. They'd left me alone with her.

I heard her close the front door. She would be coming for me. It wouldn't be long, either. My heart beat faster. I wasn't going to wait for her to corner me. I pushed the window open, shoved the screen up, and climbed out on the porch roof in my bare feet, moving slowly on the gritty shingles so I wouldn't slip. Then I inched the screen back down so she couldn't tell I'd gone out the window.

The sultry summer air hung without a breeze.

If I was fast she would never know where I'd gone. Looking over my shoulder, I climbed down the lattice on the side of the porch and fled across the grass. I couldn't make it to the lilacs. They were too far. She would see me running. I made it to the garden shed and slipped inside.

It had to be 200 degrees in there. Sweat poured out of me. There was nowhere to hide. The one room shed was a jumble of old rakes and hoes and clippers, dead flies and oil on the concrete floor, and spiders baking in the corners. I shrank against the door, cracking it so I wouldn't suffocate.

The kitchen screened door banged. I peered through the crack, holding the heavy shed door open with my sweaty hands, in time to see Janey stalking with the scissors across the grass.

Then I couldn't see her anymore. Where did she go? I kept my face in the door for air.

Bam! The shed door slammed, almost cutting off my nose.

"You let me out," I screamed, beating on the door. "I'll tell your mother and father!"

The door flew open. Janey stood there gloating with the red scissors in her fist.

"Little tattletale," she mocked. "You think they're going to believe you?"

"Get away from me! I want my mother!"

"Of course you want your mother, you little baby. But she's gone away and she's going to die."

"She is not! You're a liar!"

"She went to the hospital and she's going to die and then you're going to be a pathetic little orphan that no one wants. You'll have to live out here in the shed with the dead flies."

"You're just cruel. Let me go. You let me out of here now."

"Not until I finish your haaaiiiircut," she sang, waving the scissors.

And that's when I slipped under her chunky arm and ran for my life toward the wild hillside beyond the garden. I made it through the tomato plants and the lettuce. My monstrous cousin pounded across the grass after me, waving the scissors, yelling, "Haaaiiiircut." Finally, I made it to the lilacs, dropped to my hands and knees, and crawled into that green jungle of massive old branches. I wormed as far back as I could until I found my hiding place among those bony, entangled roots, hugging the thick trunks, silently begging the plants to protect me.

Janey ran to the edge of the lilacs, where she peered into the gloom like a troll squinting with one eye. I could see her metal teeth.

"I see you hiding in there," she taunted. "Come out for your haaaairrrcut or I'll chop down all these stupid bushes to get you."

I shrank back against the lilacs.

"Coming to get you, Frizz." She crawled after me with the red scissors, but the lilacs ripped at her long hair. "Rotten old bushes, get away from me."

I moved back again, breathing hard.

"Protect me, please, please," I whispered. "Lilacs, please, protect from this creep, lilacs, please, send her down to the deep."

"Huh, my foot's stuck!" Janey gasped.

Caught in the roots, she frantically pulled at her foot. She tried to pull her toes out of her shoe, but the ground gripped her whole foot up to the ankle. Twisting around, she dropped the red scissors. And then when she reached for the scissors, still peering through the branches at me, the Bad Thing happened.

The hillside groaned, cracked open, and swallowed her fingers. She screamed. And then the earth split open even wider into a vast, gravelike crevice, ripping back from the huge old roots, roots that suddenly looked exactly like ribs, bony arms and legs, and grasping fingers. Futilely grabbing at the dirt, Janey tumbled into the crevice. Clods of earth crumbled over her pink shorts, filling her clothes, her hair, her eyes and nose and metal mouth. She screamed again. Seconds later, the split widened. With a gasp, Janey slid further down into the dark hole, reaching out for the roots that closed over her like clacking jaws.

Slipping again, fists trying to grab something to stop her fall, she tumbled more deeply into the chasm. Then, in one horrific rumble, the earth closed over her head. She was gone. Completely gone without a trace, as if she'd never existed. The hill of ancient lilacs had devoured her.

"Uhhh, uhhhh uhhh," I gasped, my chest heaving up and down. Too terrified to move, I crouched against the roots, holding them for the longest time.

Silence. The green leaves hung in the sullen air. I almost expected to see Janey crawling out of the dirt, her fingers poking through the earth, but there was no sign of her. The sun moved down the sky. Still in shock, I had no idea how long I'd been sitting there when my aunt and uncle finally pulled up in the truck. To my relief, my mother was with them. She wasn't going to die after all. It had all been a big lie. I could see all three of them through the leaves as they slowly walked into the house.

A few minutes later, my aunt opened the screened door.

"Girls?" she called. "Janey, where are you?"

I crawled out of the lilacs, brushing the dirt off my knees.

"Here I am," I called. "I've been gardening like you asked."

Swamp Mansion and Other Dark Tales (Vol. 1)

Swamp Mansion
AC Stone

For weeks after I moved into the abandoned mansion at the edge of the swamp, I heard scratching noises along the walls. Not inside the walls, more like something moving slowly across the dry peeling wallpaper. I know what you're thinking. No, I'm not crazy.

I called an exterminator. A skinny guy in his late twenties with blurry prison tattoos and a scraggly beard showed up in a panel van. A huge plastic ant clung to the top of his rusted van. The exterminator appeared to be more comfortable hanging around with the rats, snakes, and gators in this forgotten corner of Louisiana than with people. He wasn't much of a talker at first, but he looked as if he could get the job done between smoking foul-smelling cigarettes. I guess swamp creatures could harass anyone living near the murky, stagnant waters of the bayou.

He spent about two hours poking around the dusty rooms. I could tell he thought I was crazy, but I hadn't paid him yet, so he was kind enough not to come right out and say it. He didn't have to. His eyes spoke for him.

"Nothin' here," he said with a gulp. "No rats, roaches, nothin' at all. Thought about wood-boring wasps, but no sir. Not possum. Too big. I didn't find any mice holes. And no turds. No food here. Kitchen's pert near bare. How long ya been here, sir, if ya don't mind me asking?"

I did mind. It wasn't any of his business. He didn't need to know what I was doing here or that I had moved into this abandoned plantation-style mansion just over a month ago.

"Not long," is all I said, figuring I was about to waste a wad of bills on a pointless exterminator visit. I just had to hang on and complete this renovation. My plan was to settle in, fix up the house, trim the grounds, and get it listed for sale. A quick flip would generate a bit of cash flow, which I really needed to catch up on my back alimony, but I was starting to worry that I couldn't take another month here. Maybe my imagination was getting the better of me.

He shook his head regretfully and said, "Nobody's lived here for decades. So what'd ya hear 'xactly?"

"Scratching along the walls. Sometimes the floor. Sometimes the ceiling. All around, but very faint. Most of the time, though, nothing at all."

"When d'ya hear it, day or night?"

"Night. Only when it's dark."

"Well, sir, I'm genuine sorry. Can't help ya, but we can come out and do a regular service and …"

"No," I said, cutting him off before his sales pitch got rolling. "That won't be necessary. I won't be here long."

"The sun's setting. I can wait 'til dark."

"No, no thanks," I said with as much country politeness as I could fake comfortably.

He reached though the open van door, pulled out an aluminum clipboard with invoice forms, and filled in the blanks as I waited. He looked over at my BMW with Indiana license plates as he scribbled, which meant I'd probably pay extra for the service. Then he tore off the invoice, handed it to me, and stuffed his hands into the filthy pockets of his beige overalls. I guess I had to go get my checkbook. He didn't likely take platinum cards out here in the middle of the bayou. Back on the loose gravel driveway, I started to walk back to the porch that needed stripping and a fresh coat of varnish when I read his bill.

"Seventy-nine dollars?" I asked.

"Long way. We're forty minutes from town," he replied.

"Don't you ever come out here?"

"Well, yeah, sure. But it's a ways. Look, I got some ideas…"

I waved him off and went back inside for my checkbook. Furniture draped with yellowed sheets and cobwebs filled the parlor. I heard the scratching noise again, then a slight rubbing sound like fingertips on the window glass. Then the stale-smelling room went completely silent. I looked all around and then out the front window at the cypress trees covered in Spanish moss hanging on branches above the black water. The windows were clear. Turning back, I still saw nothing on the walls, even up close.

When I returned to the driveway, I thought about taking him back inside to hear the sound, but I felt pretty certain that it wouldn't start up again. Anyway, I had explained it to him enough.

He took my out-of-state check, looked it over suspiciously, and said, "I was 'round here long ago and saw this place from a fishin' boat." He pointed toward the water at the end of the peninsula. "There's a deep spot out there that we heard about as kids. Just past that point. Good thing we were explorin' and not tryin' real hard to catch fish 'cause not even a bite. They say it's a devil's hole. Let out a hundred yards of line and didn't hit bottom."

"Limestone sinkholes is all," I said dismissively. "They're fairly common in swamps."

"The electronic depth finder couldn't tell how far it went down."

"Just a natural phenomenon."

He swatted a mosquito on his neck, which left a splotch of blood. "Most of these waters aren't over fifteen feet deep. Ya'd think the fish would like it there, being so far down and cool, but we didn't get nothin'."

"Wrong kind of bait, maybe."

He shook his head pensively as if I'd somehow insulted him. Shaking his head was his standard response to just about every observation I made that evening. He said, "I got an idea or two to help ya, but I don't want ya to get weirded out. What ya're experiencin' might be … well, paranormal."

I felt my left eyebrow rise.

He gave me the "aw shucks" look and started to fumble through his pockets. "This is just my day job. On the weekends, my friends and I check out houses that have … well, what we call activity." He handed me a black business card with eerie green lettering with only a post office box and website below the name "West Gulf Paranormal Society."

I replied, "Well, thanks anyway, but no. I'm pretty skeptical about such things."

"Yep, us too. We're lookin' for the truth, which is usually just bad electrical wiring, creaky floor joists, plain ole ordinary stuff. Four of us on the team. A historical researcher, a psychic, and the leader … and me," he added with a tinge of southern humility. "I do the tech work."

I looked at the indigo lettering of amateur tattoos on his forearms, probably the finest artwork that you could get from the Michelangelos in the state penitentiary. There was nothing on earth that was going to get me to let this guy and his gang in this mansion for the night. I said flatly, "It's not for me."

"Okay, but it don't cost ya nothin'. We got all kinds of equipment. Full spectrum cameras that see the warm spots of critters crawlin' in the walls after dark. Might just be what ya need. Nothin' there right now, but overnight, who knows?"

"I appreciate you coming out here."

"If ya change your mind, the name's Cody."

"Okay, Cody, thanks again."

He fired up the ignition to his panel van. The plastic head of the ant on the roof bobbed as the exterminator left. The tires of the van crunched the loose-gravel driveway that cut through the trees until it was out of sight.

I walked toward the cattails and pale green reeds that grew thick between the muddy banks and the slow-moving waters. The humid air made me drip with sweat, even though I had not been moving much. Gnats buzzed around my ears in a swirling cloud. Pairs of blinking eyes from submerged alligators rose just above the waterline by a fallen tree trunk halfway in and halfway out of the swamp. What was I thinking when my brother talked me into buying this rehab project? This was no place for anyone to live.

Back in the mansion, I flipped through a three-ring binder full of my hand-written notes and graph-paper sketches of how I would redo each room. A couple of estimates from roofers slid out from the inner pocket onto the musty rug. When I picked them up, my eyes caught the old archways and valences in this beautiful, dilapidated mansion from a lost century. This would have been a great house for me and my wife to move into after our wedding, well, I guess I ought to be saying my ex-wife by now. Back then, we were young and in love, not needing anything more than our dreams, even if we didn't have any real plans. Now after the lawyers, depositions, and divorce trial, all I had left were plans and not even the broken shards of a dream anymore.

I slapped the binder shut and considered painting the hallway, but it seemed more like a hammer and crowbar night to me. I pried off some wainscoting that I might be able to paint tomorrow, or perhaps I'd replace with fresh wood. When I stopped banging the hammer for a moment, I heard a sound all around me like dead leaves rustling in an icy wind. I turned around toward the hallway and saw a black shadow so dark I could not see through it. I froze, trying to make sense of the thick darkness that hung in the air and then congealed into something of a humanoid shape. The shadow figure, even hunched over, was almost as tall as the entire hallway. At first, I thought it could be a column of dark smoke, but I didn't smell fire. My eyes had to be playing tricks on me. Maybe that exterminator had sprayed something that left a cloud, but that didn't make sense either. The shadow hung motionless in the still hallway. In the silence, I struggled to understand what I was seeing. Then the black shadow grew smaller and lighter, almost to a translucent gray. It glided to the left until it disappeared into the wall. I heard the hammer slip from my hand and thud on the carpeted floor. Then the itchy, rustling sound on the wallpaper and ceiling started up again.

I ran through the front door, across the porch, and toward my car. I found Cody's business card from the West Gulf Paranormal Society in my shirt pocket and called him on my mobile device. He and his team could be there in a little more than two hours, unless tomorrow would be better. I told him tonight would be okay. Definitely tonight. I waited for them in my BMW with the headlights shining across the uncut grass of the front yard. The radio stations were mostly static, so I waited, listening to the croaking frogs and other creatures of the swamp. At 10:36 p.m., the exterminator van with the ridiculous plastic ant pulled up next to my sedan. I got out, relieved more than anything else to see another person there with me.

Cody said, "Hey, glad ya called us, Mister, um …"

"Farley," I replied, filling in his shaky memory.

"Yeah, right, of course, Mr. Farley," he said, extending his hand to shake mine. I shook his hand, and he introduced me to the two other people who had alighted from the panel van and were approaching me from my blind spot. "This is Jacob, our team leader."

Jacob did his best to smile through the greeting, but his eyes looked past me at the façade of the ramshackle mansion in the moonlight. This Jacob character had gauges in his earlobes the size of Buick hubcaps. From the way he stroked his long goatee, I guess I was supposed to take him seriously.

Jacob said, "Thank ya for letting us come out here. We've always wanted to do a full investigation of this place, but never got the invite before. This place has been abandoned my entire life. This could be amazing, but more than anything, Mr., uh, Farley, I want ya to know that we're here to help." He handed me a legal document entitled "Authorization and Release" and said, "We're gonna need your permission to film here tonight."

"This is Amanda, our psychic," said Cody the exterminator, turning slightly to a short woman who had dyed her hair a shiny magenta. Her black halter top didn't cover the multi-colored tattoos of Egyptian gods, curling snakes, and tarot cards across her shoulders and neck.

She raised her open palm to grind the introduction to a halt and said with cool detachment, "There's a Sentinel here."

I was probably more amused than anything, but didn't chuckle out loud. Amanda the psychic simply pointed out toward the peninsula that extended into the swamp where Cody the full-time exterminator and part-time ghost tech had gone fishing as a teen. Most likely I would regret it, but I had to ask, "A sentinel?"

Without making any eye contact, the psychic said to us, "Out there, hovering over the water. It seems to be fading, weakening. I'll be at the edge of the swamp for a while."

There was nothing to see out there but a slight shimmer of moonlight on the stagnant black water.

Jacob turned to Cody. "Let's set up the gear inside."

Amanda nodded to no one in particular and walked across the thick grass of the yard toward the banks of the swamp.

"A sentinel?" I asked the men as they unloaded clunky plastic suitcases from the rusted van.

Jacob explained, "A Sentinel, since you asked, is a guardian of a portal between the spirit realm and ours. Amanda is very sensitive."

I turned to Cody. "So what'd you tell her?"

"Nothing," he shrugged, "except that ya've been experiencing some activity here at the mansion. She's better off cold, without any ideas already formed. She's good, though. Real good."

"Uh-huh," I said as credulously as I could manage. "Guardians?"

"Yeah," Jacob said, "to keep spirits in their world and us out of theirs."

I whispered to Cody, "Hope they don't charge overtime. I'm on a tight budget."

Cody just smiled, not looking too sure how to reply as he slid the side door of his van shut.

I glanced down at the Authorization and Release form in my hand, not really intending to read it or sign it, but Jacob pointed at the document and said, "It's fairly standard. We good?"

Between the crazy psychic and the stupid legal document in my hand, I felt a sinking feeling in my gut. I regretted calling these clowns out here, but I had seen something in the house. There was no turning back now. I read the first couple of paragraphs and really didn't care. Maybe I just wanted, maybe just needed someone out here to convince me that I wasn't losing my mind. I scrawled my signature at the bottom of the document and gave it back to Jacob, the team leader. He stuffed it into the back pocket of his baggy shorts while Cody trudged into the mansion with arms full of black suitcases and power cords wrapped on spools.

I suppose everyone has a talent. Mine is making impulsive, boneheaded mistakes and figuring it out too late. Too bad you can't make any money off that. I'd already be retired.

Jacob and Cody asked where I saw the shadow figure, so I led them upstairs to the hallway and turned on as many lights as I could. They set up tripods and explained that the full spectrum cameras could film visible light, as well as the infrared and ultraviolet light that the human eye cannot detect, but were around us all the time. Cody showed me some handheld thermometers and some other gear I didn't understand much. He tested a couple of ordinary micro-recorders which he said were for EVPs, Electronic Voice Phenomena.

"EVPs? Really?" I asked.

"Yeah, I want to pick up this rustling, scratching sound ya hear on the walls. Maybe some spirit voices, too."

"Spirit voices?"

"Yeah, disembodied sounds."

As they finished setting up, a chunky woman perhaps in her thirties waddled up the staircase and said, "I figured I'd find you here."

Funny how I didn't hear anyone knock.

Jacob introduced her to me as Karen, their researcher.

"Sorry I'm late," Karen said, "but you're not gonna believe what I found out about this place. I stayed online at the café to check out old newspaper articles and some stories kept by the local historical society. This was a rice plantation before the Civil War. Hundreds of slaves."

"A lot of misery here," Jacob noted as he connected his cameras to a laptop computer.

"After the war," she continued, "the place fell into disrepair, and then hurricanes pounded Louisiana in the 1890s. Flooded this whole area. The rice fields were gone. Then it was all swamp. But that's not the weirdest part."

Jacob and Cody paused from fiddling with their equipment and cameras.

Karen said, "Around the 1920s and 30s, this mansion was occupied by a local man known as Jean Lefrain, supposedly some kind of voodoo priest. He was hanged for murder in 1934. The sheriff found human bones arranged ceremonially throughout the mansion and got enough of a statement to pass for a confession back then. According to local legend, this Lefrain guy practiced a ritual where he would tie a person to a tree, chop off their hands with a machete, and then slice their throats. Nobody knows how many people died here or if it's even true. Could be a local myth, but a couple of articles mentioned the story. I need more time to look into it. One article freaked me out. His last words before they tightened the noose around his neck were "You cannot hurt me. I walk between the worlds."

Jacob said, "Wow, good job, Karen. Really good stuff. Amanda ought to hear it."

Karen furrowed her brow. "Where's she at?"

"Out by the water," Jacob said, "She saw something out there. Maybe a Sentinel."

Karen nodded slightly, looking impressed. I weaved my way around the dusty, sheet-covered furniture toward a window facing the swamp. I looked for Amanda, the alleged psychic. Fast-moving clouds obscured the moonlight briefly, but I could see overgrown peninsula where she had headed a while ago. No one was out there.

"I guess she'll come in when we go dark. Ready?" Jacob asked his team.

Karen had picked up a video camera and mounted it on her shoulder. Apparently she was more than the team's researcher. She said, "Video ready. You want me to tape an introduction, Jacob?"

"No," he replied. "Let's do an intro after we see what's here, if anything. Fits better."

"Copy that," she replied like a pilot talking to some control tower.

Cody the exterminator said, "I'm good, too. EVP recorders, check. Full spectrum cameras, check. Got all four on line. Temperature gauges, check. We're a go."

"Let's go dark. You got it, Cody?" Jacob asked, but it was more of a command than a question.

"Yup," he replied, checking his flashlight. "That old fuse box is back near the kitchen. It'll only take me a sec to throw the switch." Cody bounded down the long central staircase at the end of the hallway out of sight.

"What's this 'going dark'?" I asked Jacob, who fidgeted with the volume button on a black walkie-talkie.

Jacob said, "We shut off all the lights. Make the place as dark as possible. You know, for gathering evidence. Entities are more likely to manifest themselves if all the artificial lighting, well, at least most of it, is off. We try to minimize electrical currents during an investigation, except for our cameras and equipment." He clicked his flashlight on and off and then dropped it into the pocket of his baggy shorts.

"Hang on," I said. "I don't have a flashlight."

"You won't need one. We'll be right here with you."

Cody's voice crackled on Jacob's walkie-talkie. "I'm at the fuse box."

"Throw it," Jacob replied with his walkie-talkie right up to his mouth, and with that, every light in the mansion went off. I felt my pulse in my chest and neck as my eyes adjusted to the blackness of the mansion.

Jacob and Cody focused on their computer screens, which gave the room a faint blue glow, but not enough to illuminate more than a few feet from their table. I heard the low buzz of the generator that powered their equipment out in the van. Cody walked toward the hallway waving a hand-held thermometer from floor to ceiling and side to side. We watched him on the computer screens, because once he slipped into the darkness, we couldn't see him. When he returned, there were no unusual readings. A steady seventy-four degrees measured throughout the hall.

Jacob took an EVP recorder and tried to speak with the spirits in the mansion, asking them to communicate with him, tell him why they were still here, show him a sign. He asked them to knock or do anything at all. The dark rooms were still and silent. Only the chirps of crickets in the distant swamp and the rumble of the generator outside made any background noise. Nothing more. I guessed that I had gotten what I wanted out of this exercise in futility. The divorce, being broke, living alone in this freaked-out mansion for a month had really done it. I'd completely lost it. Gone off the deep end. Now I needed to figure out how to get these so-called paranormal investigators back on the road. Fortunately, even they were sounding a bit frustrated.

Karen lowered her video camera. "I don't hear anything on the walls. No scratching noise that was reported."

Cody said, "Nothing detected by the microphones or the full spectrum cams."

Jacob asked his team, "Does Amanda have a walkie-talkie?"

Cody replied, "Naw, I hadn't broken 'em out yet when she started outside."

"She's done this before," Karen said. "Remember back at the Bogalusa Asylum? She was gone most the night."

"Okay," Jacob said, "but when I take a break, I'll look for her." He turned toward me, which I could tell more by the directness of his voice than by his face, which the darkness concealed. "Now then, Mr. Farley, whereabouts were you when you saw the shadow entity?"

"Over there," I pointed before realizing no one could see my hand. I guessed I could play along a little longer, taking short, tentative steps toward the wall where I had pulled off the wainscoting. "I was standing right here."

Jacob took confident strides toward me and directed me to move to the exact spot where the shadow entity had appeared. That was about the last place I was going to stand.

He said, "It's a little unusual to have the homeowner here during an investigation, but it streamlines things. You've been great so far. If what you've been experiencing has a natural explanation, well, we'll find out. Give you an explanation. How 'bout standin' there a few minutes and we'll see."

If it would get these guys to pack up and go, I could tolerate a few minutes of this, but not long. I stepped cautiously down the dark hall, already regretting it.

Cody said, "Hold there, Mr. Farley. Um, Jacob, his heat signature is throwing off the cameras, so I need a while to adjust them."

"Okay," Jacob said. "Let's us know when we're back on."

"We're good," replied Cody.

I stood there for a few long minutes, hands flat against my sides far from the walls. Chilly air drifted from behind me onto my shoulders, and I felt the muscles in my back tighten. I turned around. Nothing was there. The air wasn't just chilly, it was downright cold. Cody and Jacob looked up from their computer screens at me. Their eyes were wide and unblinking.

Jacob said to me, "Do you sense anything around you?"

"Cold," I replied. "Just cold."

"Where? All around you or …?"

"No, mostly to my left. What's going on?" I started to step toward them and the faint light cast by their computer screens.

"Wait, wait," Jacob said in a stern whisper. "Just hold there a minute. That's all. I promise."

"Guys, I'm not into this. I got to get …"

"Please, just a sec. You're not in any danger," Jacob said, not very convincingly.

Cody focused on his computers, the whites of his eyes visible in the pale blue light of the screens. He said, "It's getting bigger. Right at the cold spot."

I looked to my left, seeing only the walls and the dim shadows cast by peeling strips of wallpaper.

"It's almost like it's arced over him, on the left," Jacob observed as he glanced from the laptop to me and back. "I wish we could get a thermometer to him."

Cody grabbed something on the table and started to stand up when Jacob said, "No, no, we could scare it off."

That was enough. More than enough. I walked straight toward Karen, who followed me with the lens of the video camera. I flipped the wall switch up and down, but the room remained dark. I guess I'd forgotten that the exterminator cut the electricity.

"Guys," I said, "I think we're done. I don't know what's going on here, but we're done. I'm going to sell this place as soon as possible, as is."

Jacob exhaled slowly, apparently trying to gather his thoughts and pretend to be patient with me. I could see that coming, but I was finished.

The team leader said, "We just filmed, well, something with the thermal camera. Not visible light, but coldness. The outline of something human-shape, well, kinda. It was standing right next to you. We could see the temperature differences and a distinct body."

Cody said, "It got bigger. Then it faded away when ya moved. Could be that Sentinel."

"Here's an idea, guys. Send me the tape, but I'm outta here. We're all outta here."

"Okay, okay," Jacob said, "It's your call. I respect that. We'd like to stay, with your permission. But before you go, look at what we captured."

I said, "I'd feel a lot better about it if there were some lights on. I can't see anything in here."

Cody ignored my request, tapped on the laptop, and said, "Here's where it started."

Jacob, Cody, and I watched the screen as Karen continued filming us. A red light atop her camera was all I could make out of her on the far wall. Images on the computer screen began to move. I could see the outline of a person, presumably me, with a dark red core and head, but the rest of my body appeared in oranges and yellows. The hallway behind me and the walls appeared as dark blues, almost black. Then I could see a tall, distorted cloud shape forming next to me. It seemed to tighten and pull together into the shape of a large person, but not exactly. When I walked quickly toward the camera, the shape next to me faded and disappeared.

Jacob quietly said to Cody, "That's excellent. Good enough to pitch a pilot episode."

None of the team showed any signs of leaving anytime soon, and there wasn't much chance of me walking through the dark mansion with the power cut. I have to admit I was intrigued and, yeah, I'll admit it, I was scared. As the investigators worked their equipment, I paused to listen to the old house. The crickets out in the swamp had stopped chirping. No frogs croaked. Then everyone looked in the direction of the dark hallway. We all heard it at once. First a slight rubbing sound, then scratching noises that grew louder and soon seemed to be all around us on the walls and the ceiling. Whatever they were, they were moving. There were a lot of them.

Jacob and Cody shone their flashlights all around the parlor and hallway, but the walls were empty.

Jacob said, "You hear that, right?"

Karen and Cody both said, "Yeah," their voices quavering.

So maybe I wasn't crazy after all.

Jacob moved back to the computers and leaned over Cody. "You're recording all this?"

"Got the audio. What is it?"

"Don't know," he replied.

Karen said in a hushed tone, "Amazing."

"Keep that camera rolling," Jacob said to her. "Especially down that corridor."

"Copy that," Karen replied.

The scratching noises were getting closer to us. Adrenaline surged through me as we waited for someone or something to appear, but we didn't see anything. Then Cody pointed to his monitor and called out, "The infrared. Check out what the full spectrum cam is picking up in infrared."

Jacob and I looked over his shoulder at the images of the hallway. Pale green oval shapes were moving slowly along the dark walls and ceiling. Jacob went over to Karen so she could film him in action. He shone his flashlight around the room again while she tracked his beam of light. Still nothing showed up on the peeling wallpaper.

He whispered, "Cody, can you focus in on one of those shapes with the infrared camera?"

"I'll try." Cody tapped the keys until a single blurred pale green image filled the entire screen. With a few more adjustments, it came into focus—a transparent human hand cut off above the wrist. The hand crawled slowly across the wall with the deliberate movements of a prowling tarantula. Its fingers and thumb dragged the severed arm along the hallway, into the parlor, and then onto the ceiling where the angle prevented Cody's camera from tracking it.

I had to get out of this mansion right now, but the stairs to the first floor were in total darkness. There was no way I was getting stuck in this place alone, lost in huge rooms and winding corridors where I couldn't see anything. My heart throbbed throughout my entire body to the point where I couldn't think straight, but I figured I was better off with these other people than fumbling alone through this huge house in the dark.

Cody said, "There are dozens of these apparitions all around us. Dozens of severed hands."

"I can hear them," Karen said, "but can't film them with the video camera."

"Then keep it on us," ordered Jacob. "Cody, you got other cameras to pick up infrared?"

"Yeah," he replied. "Got cams in two other rooms and one on the front yard where Amanda saw something over the swamp."

"Check 'em," Jacob ordered.

"Nothing on the first floor, either room. I got something on the front lawn, though."

"Let's see."

Cody focused the outdoor camera and zoomed in at the edge of the water. Hundreds of pale green images emerged from the swamp. He increased the focus and I could see severed hands creeping onto the land like a hoard of spiders.

I yelled, "Listen! All of you! We've got to get out of here." The hands were all headed toward the mansion.

Jacob said sharply to me, "Look, this is the most incredible thing we've ever seen. We're getting it on film. We can't bail now."

Then the small amount of light cast by the computer screens and their equipment went out. No one could see anything. I inched my way over to the window and surveyed the front yard. The generator out in the exterminator's panel van was silent. The entire mansion was completely dark.

Jacob said, "We gotta get power back on. Cody, get that generator going again."

The three investigators bolted down the staircase with their flashlights before I could turn away from the window and go with them. I was alone in the dark parlor. The rasping sounds on the walls grew stronger and closer to me, so I stepped as best I could in the direction of the stairs, stretching my arms out in front of me. I bumped my knee into some kind of furniture, which I had to go around. There had been an antique sofa there, not far from the stairwell. I was getting closer to the steps.

"Hey, guys!" I yelled.

No one answered.

I tried again, "Hey!"

I could only hear the scratching sounds of the severed ghost hands moving across the walls. I stepped as quickly as I could, not caring anymore if I slammed into furniture or anything else. I moved faster now that my eyes were adjusting to the blackness. I barely saw the handrail of the stairs, but I grabbed it, and worked my way down to the first floor, where I knew the house well enough to get to the front door.

The moon cast some light on the porch, the driveway, and the cars. The investigators would be at the panel van, trying to get the generator started again. I ran to the van. The sliding side door was open.

No one was there.

"Cody? I called out. "Jacob?"

No one replied.

"Hey," I tried again. "Um, Karen? Anybody?"

The swamp was silent. My BMW was right next to the van. My car keys were in my pants pocket. I was getting out of there, but these investigators should be around somewhere. I cursed under my breath. Where could they be? They had just left the mansion minutes before I did.

I pressed the button on my key fob to unlock the car doors. My headlights came on, illuminating the driveway and part of the front yard. Toward the edge of the grass was a dead flashlight.

"Where are you guys?" I said in a panicked whisper, my choked voice no longer able to yell loudly. My heart was pounding. I felt a cold sweat trickle down my back despite the muggy heat of the night.

Again, no reply. I stepped toward the flashlight on the ground. Karen's video camera was a few feet from it in the weeds, as if she'd simply tossed it there. No red light glowed atop her recorder. I surveyed the rest of the gravel driveway, at least what I could see in headlights. The loose stones had been churned up in spots. Deep lines were etched in the stone driveway as if something had just dragged heavy things across it.

Nothing made sense anymore. I could call the team from my car, unless I left my mobile device inside the mansion. It didn't matter. I reached for the door handle on the driver's side. I had to.

Then a cold, bony hand grabbed the back of my neck.

I spun around. No one was behind me. The grip on my neck tightened.

Instantly I put both on my hands on the back of my neck, but there was nothing there—only the feeling of the icy hand holding onto me. I tried to throw off whatever was gripping my neck, but my empty hands slid off my bare neck.

Then I felt another hand seize my forearm. I quickly turned my arm toward the headlights. The impressions of four fingers and a palm pressed into my skin. I freaked out, trying to scrape off the invisible hand with my own hand, but that didn't work.

Then another hand latched onto the back of my thigh. I turned around and started to run, sprint away from there. No, I had to get into the car. A ghost hand covered my mouth. I couldn't see anything there, just the sensation of a cold hand sealing my mouth shut. Then dozens of invisible hands gripped my body. I tried to wrestle myself free, but it was no use.

The invisible hands clamped down and slammed me onto the jagged stones of the driveway. I struggled to turn, pull away, fight them off somehow. The ghost hands covered my entire body and dragged me slowly across the lawn. I held onto tufts of grass, but the moist soil came loose. I dug my fingers into the ground as hard as I could, but the invisible hands continued to pull me across the yard. I was heading toward the peninsula and the deep hole far out in the swamp.

I couldn't scream for help, but I tried anyway. The invisible hand across my mouth was too tight.

My last chance was at the edge of the water. I grabbed as many tall reeds and cattails as I could with both arms and hugged them with all my strength as the adrenaline surged through me. I sensed that if I could hold on, maybe the hands would release me. The hands tightened their clasp and squeezed my entire body. They tugged harder and harder, thrashing and twisting me as I sank into the soft putrid mud. Soon the water was up to my face. The long reeds sliced through my palms and forearms like swords, but somehow I held on firmly. The invisible hands relented and relaxed their grip. Dry land was only a few feet away.

Then with a jolt, the ghost hands yanked me away from the muddy bank and pulled me under the black swamp water.

Lure of the Owl

KM Rockwood

Liz gathered the blankets more closely around her frail chest and stared determinedly at the TV. For the umpteenth time this week, a Halloween special, *Dread Creatures of the Night,* was showing. A vampire bat filled the screen.

If they'd let her get cable in this room, like in her old room, she wouldn't have to watch the same thing over and over.

Across the room, Maddie gathered up the lunch tray with its congealed stew and untouched milk. She sighed. "You didn't eat your lunch, Aunt Liz. You have to eat something."

No, she didn't. Not when she was pretty sure they were trying to poison her. Maddie thought she was going to inherit the house. Wouldn't she be surprised.

The visiting nurse looked from the tray to Liz. "Are you not hungry?" she asked. "Or is there something else you'd rather eat?"

Maddie gave a harsh laugh. "She thinks we're trying to poison her."

"Sometimes chunks, like the stew, make food hard to eat," the nurse said. She reached into her bag and pulled out a pudding cup. "Will you try to eat a little of this, Liz?"

Liz glanced over at her as she pulled the cover off the cup. *It had been sealed and in the nurse's bag. Maddie might not have had a chance to get to it.*

"What kind is it?" Liz croaked, hardly recognizing her own raspy voice. Her mouth was very dry, and she hadn't tried to say anything in several days.

"Butterscotch," the nurse said.

Butterscotch. A favorite. And she was hungry.

The nurse dipped a plastic spoon in the cup, got a bit on the tip, and brought it up to Liz's mouth.

She licked her lips, then opened her mouth. She nibbled it off the spoon. The pudding tasted wonderful.

The nurse repeated the motion with a bigger spoonful. Liz let the pudding slide around in her mouth, savoring its smooth sweetness. Before she knew it, the pudding was gone.

"There. Wasn't that good?" the nurse asked.

"Yes." Liz's tongue was no longer so dry, and her voice sounded almost normal.

The nurse peered at the TV. "What're you watching?"

"A show about night creatures," Liz said. "It's been on every day lately."

"Probably because it's almost Halloween."

Liz moved her hand to touch the remote control. "Did you know that an owl hooting outside the window means that someone is going to die soon?"

"Indeed?"

"Yes. And some people think the souls of dead people come back as owls."

"Is that so?"

"Uh huh. And there's been a hoot owl right outside my window for the last few nights."

The nurse shivered. "Why do you watch that show? It must scare you."

It did, but Liz was not going to admit it. "Not really. It's just old wives' tales."

The nurse picked up her bag. "That's probably enough food for now, if she hasn't been eating," she said to Maddie. "Smooth foods—milkshakes, puddings, applesauce, mashed potatoes—that's probably the best kind of thing to feed her. Or some cans of those nutritional drinks. You can open one in front of her so she can see they're fresh. They might work better."

Liz turned her head to watch Maddie. The woman's face was frozen in a stubborn grimace. So much for the idea of sealed nutritional drinks.

"How're you sleeping?" the nurse asked Liz.

"Fine."

"No, she doesn't sleep much," Maddie said, "and she has nightmares when she does sleep. Probably because of all those stupid TV shows."

"Well, you do have some sleeping pills to give her, don't you?" the nurse asked. "I know the doctor prescribed them. Did you get the prescription filled?"

Maddie looked down at the floor. "Yes."

No one had said anything to Liz about sleeping pills. At least that she remembered.

"She doesn't like to take any of her meds," Maddie was saying. "She thinks we're trying to poison her."

Well, they were.

The nurse turned to Liz. "When your family brings your meds, you have to take them. Ask to examine them if you're afraid they've been tampered with. That should be pretty obvious. But your family is just trying to take good care of you and make you comfortable."

Right. They were waiting for her to die so they could take all her things.

Sure enough, the supper Maddie brought up was a cold salad with slimy pasta, mushy raw vegetables and some kind of smelly meat. She plunked it down on the table next to Liz's bed.

It smelled of broccoli. Liz wrinkled her nose, but she didn't look at Maddie or the food. She continued to stare at the TV, which was showing a cartoon version of the Legend of Sleepy Hollow.

Maddie shrugged and left the room, closing the door firmly behind her. It made a snicking noise.

Did it lock when she closed it?

After a while, she pulled her walker over and struggled out of bed. The bare wooden floors were cold on her feet, but she knew how difficult it would be to try to find her comfy slippers and get her feet into them. Using the bathroom took the best part of a half hour, and by the time she got back into her room, another show was on, this one with werewolves.

Moving carefully, she grabbed the tray and moved it across the room to the dresser, next to the framed picture of Jeremy. How angry Maddie would be if she spilled the food! This had been her home for years, long before Maddie and her family moved in, and she used to have the roomy master bedroom with the soft carpeting. But she'd had so many accidents—both spilling food and not making it to the bathroom in time—that they'd moved her. It was too hard to get the stains and the smells out of the carpet.

Now she stayed in the drafty room under the eaves that had been intended for a maid when the house was built over a century ago. It was small, but at some point, a bathroom had been added, so it worked better. From Maddie's point of view.

By the time Maddie came up to get the supper tray, Liz was back in bed, the blankets pulled tightly around her. The TV was showing wolves howling in the night.

Maddie took the remote control and shut off the TV. "I brought you a sleeping pill."

Lips pressed firmly together, Liz continued to stare at the blank screen.

"Now, come on." Maddie sighed. "You heard what the nurse had to say. When we bring you your meds, you have to take them." She held out her hand. Not one but two tiny white pills lay in the middle of her palm. "And I brought you a bottle of water so there's no way anyone could have put anything in it. You can watch me open it." She made an elaborate show of twisting off the cap.

It could have been opened before and the top just screwed back on, Liz thought. But a good night's sleep would be a Godsend. She took the two pills from Maddie's hand and put them on the back of her tongue. Then she reached for the water bottle and took a long drink. It moistened her dry mouth and throat, and felt good.

"Do you want me to help you get to the bathroom?" Maddie asked.

"No, thank you," Liz answered. *That would give Maddie a chance to push her down. If she ever broke her hip, she would never get out of bed again.*

Maddie shrugged. "Suit yourself. But if you do wet the bed, there's a pad with a waterproof backing under the bottom sheet. We wouldn't want you to ruin the mattress."

Liz had no intention of wetting the bed.

Putting the remote control on the dresser, Maddie managed to knock the frame with the old photograph to the floor. The glass smashed.

Staring at the frame on the floor, Liz said, "You broke Jeremy's picture!"

"Only the glass is broken," Maddie said, picking up the photo. "This is just a cheap drugstore frame. I'll get you a new one next time I'm at the store." She peered at the picture.

"That's Jeremy. My husband." Unbidden, the words tumbled out of Liz's mouth. "We were going to start a family as soon as he got back from the war." She squeezed her eyes shut tight to hold back the tears. "But he never made it back."

"Well, at least he certainly left you well off," Maddie said. "This big house and lots of money. You've never wanted for anything."

That's an odd way to put it. She'd 'wanted' for Jeremy her entire adult life.

Maddie put the picture back on the dresser. She didn't bother to clean up the bits of broken glass. Liz would have to be very careful when she got up to go to the bathroom in the night. Maddie reached over and opened the window.

"Please leave it shut," Liz said. "That hoot owl will be back. He'll keep me awake."

"The fresh air will do you good. It gets so stuffy in here. And since you've taken your pills, I bet you'll sleep right through any number of owls hooting outside the window."

She turned out the light and left.

Liz slipped down in the bed, her eyes still shut tight against the tears.

With a flurry of wings, the owl arrived. He perched on a branch right outside the window. The country folk called them eight-hooters, and claimed that they were saying, "Who cooks for you? Who cooks for you?" But Liz knew this one was calling her name. "E-liz-a-beth! E-liz-a-beth!"

Was the owl here to let her know that she was going to die soon?

The sleeping pills must be working. Instead of lying awake, listening to the owl, Liz found herself drifting off to sleep. She was surprised to realize she felt relaxed and warm. Comfortable.

Did dying feel like this? Just a comfortable drifting off?

She woke with a start when something brushed against her face, then settled against it. Her first thought was that it was the owl, come to get her, but she could still hear it outside the window. The taste and smell of musty fabric filled her mouth and nose.

Liz tensed and tried to sit up, but whatever was pressing against her face held her down. She willed her hands to lift to push it away, but her arms wouldn't move.

A voice, muffled by the thing over her face, said, "Die, you old biddy. Die! You have nothing to live for anyhow."

Maddie's voice.

She couldn't breathe, but somehow, breathing didn't seem to be very important. Like eating. Both were things people normally did, and both were essential to life. But right now, not important. Liz felt her body relax.

Then she didn't feel her body anymore. Or rather, her body felt very different. A cool wind ruffled her feathers. Sitting otherwise very still, she turned her head and looked at the owl perched beside her on the branch.

"Jeremy?" she asked.

"Elizabeth. Yes, it's me. I've come to take you away. It's All Hallow's Eve. The gates of heaven and hell are flung open tonight."

"And where are we going?"

Although it came out as a hoot, Liz knew Jeremy was laughing. "Heaven, of course, my dear."

Together, the two owls spread their wings and flew into the night.

Old Man Shotgun
BG House

Bobby took the empty Coca-Cola bottle and set it down sideways on the mossy stump of a tree behind Sylvia's split-level house. He grabbed it with his pinkish, pudgy hand and spun it with a quick twist of his wrist. It swung around, pointing first to Stevie, then to Sylvia, then to Bobby, then me, and around again and again. Finally, the bottle decided the fate of two of the players. The open end pointed to Sylvia and the bottom pointed to Bobby.

"All right," Bobby crowed. "Let's fuck."

"Ewwwwww," Sylvia and I screamed in unison. I couldn't believe what I'd heard. I knew what it meant, and thanks to my beagle Peanuts and the neighborhood mutt that visited our garage one day, I knew just how it was done. However, Sylvia and I both figured that it was something that we weren't going to be doing with Bobby or Stevie that night or any other night.

It was summer and school was out. Woodstock would be "The Happening." Charles Manson and the Family would commit horrible murders. Apollo 11 would put a man on the Moon. Honky-Tonk Woman was in the top ten hits. Troll dolls were all the rage. And a short, bucktoothed, ten-year-old girl would discover true friendship and how to stare horror in the face.

June 1969 and I was that girl with the mousy, tangled brown hair and squinty hazel eyes. I thought the world was a gas. I spent every day at the swimming pool and every night sneaking out of my house. I wasn't alone. I had friends, Sylvia, Stevie, and Bobby. Our bikes were our steeds. We went everywhere together. The neighborhood with the Chesapeake tidal canal was our hangout. Nothing was off limits as far as we could peddle, even the 7-Eleven on the busy highway. A dare was a dare. A bet was a bet, and our word was worth the spit we sealed it with.

My pals were tops. Sylvia was stunning. She had waist-length, straight blond hair, perfect teeth, an already curvy body, and lanky legs. Her mom always treated me special … kind of like I was pitiful or something, but I didn't care. She was really nice and pretty, too. Tall, athletic Stevie had rusty-colored hair. He lived next door to me with his two older brothers. I thought he was so cute, you could bet that I'd never tell him. Then there was Bobby, the freckle-faced preacher's son who sported a brown buzz cut. He could be a real hothead, too. He even already smoked Camel cigarettes that he stole from his dad.

We were tight. If one of us got grounded, the others would come to the house and sit outside the open window and keep the captive company. That's just what you did. We took care of each other. One night in particular would test this alliance.

***

It was a hot and sticky day. My father packed me and my brother and sisters up into his powder-blue VW Bug and dropped us off at the Officers Club pool for a day of swimming like every other day. Then, once we were home, I had to check in on my drunken mother and make dinner, all while my dad turned his attention to his martinis. After about the sixth one, he was blotto! I knew I wouldn't be missed. You know, Dragnet was much more interesting than me. So, I went into my bedroom, removed the screen, and just climbed out the one-story window.

I met up with the gang at the bottom of the street in the cul-de-sac. Sylvia and I rode our Schwinns with the bells and purple and pink streamers dangling from the handlebars. Stevie and Bobby both rode Stingrays.

"Whatcha have for dinner?" Stevie asked.

"Chicken and dumplings and my mama's apple pie," Bobby boasted.

"Steak and some fries," Stevie said, rubbing his stomach.

"We had this thing called fondue. It was cool," Sylvia said, mimicking dipping into a fondue pot.

"I had beans and weenies and cherry Jell-O," I said. It was one of the only things I knew how to cook and the word cooking was a stretch.

Next, we told the stories of our day. Sylvia had gone to horse riding camp. Bobby hung out while his preacher dad wrote some sermons, and Stevie worked at his dad's grocery store in town, earning some summer money stacking vegetables. I'd gone to the pool and when I was home, I watched my mother to make sure she didn't drink and drive or something stupid like that.

When we finally got around to what we were going to do that night, we agreed on which direction we'd head out to first. I always wanted to go to the end of the canal where it entered the bay. There was a small strip of beach where we could see all the lights of the bridge. There was a large driftwood log that we climbed on and played Star Trek. But tonight, I was overruled. We were off to the construction site where our new elementary school was being built.

We peddled north to the dead end street and off the pavement onto a rutty dirt road. After a distance, the road forked in front of us. One way went to the construction site, the other to the lime pond junkyard, the old railroad station, and the farm. We took the fork to the construction site. When we got there, we were surprised that they had already finished the outside walls.

"We could go inside and write crap on the chalkboards," Bobby submitted for approval.

"That's so lame, it's too dark, and there's no chalkboards, you turd," Stevie said, punching Bobby in the arm.

"Well, I'm just so bored," Sylvia said, brushing a strand of her hair over her shoulder. That got the boys' attention. Keeping Sylvia's attention was first on their agenda.

"Let's go back and head out to the old railroad station," Stevie decided for us.

"Yeah, last one there's a two-headed moron," I blurted. And we rode down the dirt road as fast as we could, hitting puddles and bumps, testing our bike skills. Bobby was last and the two-headed moron.

The railroad station was really old and attempts by the grown-ups to board it up had been useless. The local teenagers went there to play chicken on the tracks, smoke pot, and make out. We came to play hide and seek and dare each other to jump off the roof all the way over the tracks and onto the gravel road. Bobby was the only one dumb enough to try and he'd ended up with a rusty rail pin in his left foot earlier that spring. Boy, did his dad get hot … had to pay for a tetanus shot and everything. But that night, we just pushed each other around on the baggage wagon and put our ears to the rail to hear if a train was coming.

"Well, it's still really pretty early, who wants to sneak up to Old Man Shotgun's farm?" Sylvia asked in a hushed voice.

The farm, at night, now that was something we actually hadn't tried before. After all, that crazy farmer usually shot rock salt at us when we rode up to his property in the daytime. Just imagine what he might do at night.

"Who's game?" Stevie asked.

"I'll go," Bobby said.

"You'll go to your own funeral," I said, realizing how stupid that sounded.

"Come on, let's go," Sylvia said, walking back to her bike.

"You coming?" they asked. I nodded and hopped on my bike, circling until everyone was mounted. It was still sort of light around 8:00 p.m.

***

We rode in a line, like four horsemen riding into Dodge in Gunsmoke. As we reached the farm, the sagging gate hung lopsided on its hinges. There was stillness in the air and it smelled of dead stuff everywhere. Flies buzzed us from every side.

"Barf-O-Matic," Bobby said, sticking his index finger down his throat.

We got off our bikes and laid them on their sides, looking into the first thing we came to. Inside, there was a swollen, old sow with maggots coming out of her eye sockets, lying rotting in the pigpen. The inside of the pen had gouges in the wood. It looked like the pigs had tried to eat their way out. Next, there were the leftovers of a chestnut mare lying bare-boned in her paddock.

"What the hell happened here?" Stevie gasped. "It looks like they all starved to death."

"I don't know but it ain't cool," Bobby said, almost white as a ghost now. Sylvia and I rubbed our hands on our shorts, trying to get rid of the slimy feeling of the rickety pen.

Warily, we approached the house, peered into the windows, and saw nothing but garbage and dead flies strewn about. It was a terrifying and thrilling sight. What happened to the farmer?

"I heard that Old Man Shotgun got sent to an insane asylum," Steve whispered.

"My parents heard from the police that he just disappeared and just left the farm alone," Bobby countered.

"Maybe we'll find a spaceship with aliens or robots … something that would explain where the old man went," I said.

Stevie wiggled his fingers in front of me and said "do-do-do-do-do-do-do-do …" It was his best Twilight Zone imitation.

"You know, this really wasn't a good idea, I mean, it's getting real dark and we don't even know what we're looking at," Bobby huffed, almost out of breath.

The streetlights on the bridge crossing the canal lit up the farm buildings. As the lights flickered, the odor of decay mixed with the stench of brackish water became overwhelming. We walked silently around the pens until we overheard an eerie *muroo, muroo, muroo* like an animal in pain. Listening carefully, we tried to find where it was coming from. I grabbed Sylvia's arm for reassurance as we went around to the back of the house and down to the waterfront. Finally, we discovered that the noise of the crying animals was just old rowboats lolling with the current, rubbing up against the wharf.

***

With a sigh of relief, we walked around to investigate the rest of the farm. No hint of Old Man Shotgun anywhere. We went to the chicken coop and found dead chickens everywhere. We headed toward the barn. It looked even bigger and darker by night. We peeked in with our faces right at the edge of the half-opened door. No sign of anyone. So, we each took a step farther until we were inside under the hayloft. Slivers of light from the bridge streamed through the cracks in the wallboards. Mayonnaise jars full of nuts and bolts and odds and ends lined the shelves. Saws, scythes, and other things were hanging from the loft along with a whole bunch of very sharp butchering tools. Everything swayed lightly in the breeze, tools clanging as they hit each other.

Stevie was the first to wander deeper into the barn. He went past mounds of moldy hay, smelling of decayed grass, and came to a fruit crate with an oil lamp on it.

"Hey Bobby, gimme a stupid match," Stevie said, as he lifted up the hazy glass dome that covered the wick of the lamp. Bobby, who was already smoking at ten, had some matches and tossed over the book.

After Stevie struck a few matches, one finally ignited. He lit the lamp. The flash of light cast chilling shadows, making us each look at least twelve feet tall.

"Look, what's that behind you," Sylvia whispered, making me jump, so I turned and it was just an old shovel. I glared at her with a look of "I'll get you back."

Almost immediately, we heard creaking and thudding coming from the bales of musty hay. Stevie spun around, swinging the lamp wildly toward the sounds. The massive shadow of a huge man with a pitchfork reflected on the wall and grew bigger and bigger. Bobby, who thought he was a real tough guy but really was just a fat kid with a flat top, yanked Stevie's arm and with one quick motion, Stevie let go of the handle and down went the lamp onto the hay.

The four of us stared in disbelief as the fire licked the floor and began to spread like spilled water. The flames snaked around Stevie, jumped over a bale of hay, and leaped up the workbench. We tried to stomp it out, but the fire had too much hay to burn. Everything in the barn was just tinder. As the bales caught and burned, we just knew we couldn't put the fire out. Screaming, we turned and ran out of the barn.

But something made us return. We thrust our heads into the barn as the fire growled and gigantic, grisly shadows covered the walls.

I stood just at the door, mesmerized by the scene. The tops of the silhouettes rose up to the rafters, bobbing and weaving with each completed circle. Malformed, starving bodies curved into the corners, across the walls, over the saws and meat hooks. Each outline produced a floating mass with pointed ears, a snout, and a curly tail. The starving pigs spun and spun, faster and faster, like a carousel of past porcine carnage. My eyes were riveted to the sight.

The flame-licked flying pigs groaned an eerie song: *"Pigs and Slop, Pigs and Slop, Old Man Shotgun's left to rot,"* over and over, faster and faster, at a dizzying rate, *"Boars and Sows, Mares and Cows, Old Man Shotgun's death we vowed."*

The smell of smoke and fire consuming Old Man Shotgun's barn engulfed me.

I couldn't move. I wanted to go in and feel the heat for myself. The fire-lit porkers howled and snorted. My eyes welled up with tears from the smoldering fumes and my face began to feel the flames licking at the hayloft. The flies that swarmed around the dead animals now crackled in the flames. The smoke almost smelled of barbeque. Starved to death. How could that man do that to his animals? Were these distorted dancing pig shadows catching me up in their siren song?

I began to weep. I took the shovel, scorching hot to the touch, and hurled it into the barn, trying to stab the burning lamp. I looked at Sylvia next to me, who had tears streaming down her face. Bobby was standing behind us, his freckled face crimson red from the firelight. No one said a word. By this time, the inferno had swallowed up the barn. Gray and black smoke shot high up into the sky and the whole farm glowed as if it were charcoal embers.

Finally, I felt a hand on my arm pulling me out of the barn.

"Holy shit, we're in real trouble now! Let's get out of here, before the cops come," Stevie said with power. We jumped on our bikes, turning around only to see the barn fully ablaze. We peddled as fast as we could, splitting up at the beginning of the paved road and the sidewalk.

Arriving at my house, I could hear the sirens and see fire trucks heading toward the farm. I hoped that they would get there soon enough to save the barn. I mean, we didn't mean to set fire to it. We'd just wanted to poke around.

***

I was still in my bed at 9:00 a.m. hoping the day would just pass me over and all would be well. I skipped breakfast and was as quiet as a mouse. Suddenly, a knock sounded on the front door. My father, nursing a hangover with a Bloody Mary, answered the door. There was a pause of about five minutes and then I heard my first and middle names bellowed from the living room. When you hear both names, you're in bigtime trouble. Feeling my heart race, I dragged my heels, ran down the hall and stopped dead when I saw a large, broad-shouldered man dressed in a dark blue uniform standing with his hands on his hips. I quickly realized he was an official fireman and I was in a truckload of trouble.

"So, young lady, what can you tell me about the fire over at the farm down the way?" the fireman asked.

"I don't know, I mean, we didn't mean it, I mean, we just went there to look …" I stuttered. I could see my father's eyes like laser beams staring a hole into me.

"Can you tell me who "we" are? It will make things go lighter on you if you tell the truth, it always does."

"It was just, you know, the guys, Bobby, Stevie, and Sylvia. We didn't mean to do anything." Tears rolled down my hot cheeks as I looked down at my shoes. I was a dirty rat.

After the tongue-lashing I received from the fireman, I figured they felt I'd learned my lesson, only my father didn't feel that way at all.

"YOU, go get the belt," he roared.

"Yes, sir," I said reluctantly. By this time, he was really steaming. I walked with my head down and sheepishly entered his bedroom. There, hanging on the rusty nail, was the dreaded belt.

"Bend over, you little fucking fire-starter, you'll pay for what you've done," my father barked as I bent over his bed and braced myself. The four-inch wide, camo-green pistol belt with rows of metal belt holes was my punishment. My father wailed on me until his arm got tired. Then, he sent me to my room where I sat there for the rest of the day, contemplating how to run away so my friends wouldn't find me. But, I knew that they were paying as well.

There was no dinner for me that night. My father was back into his martinis by three. At seven, I couldn't stay inside any longer. I had to face up to ratting out my best friends. When I met with them, we all talked so fast that none of us could understand each other.

"My mom yelled at me and told me how I worried her being so close to the fire," Sylvia said, still sniffling.

"My parents are in D.C. but my brothers thought it was really a dumb thing to do but they didn't know what to do but wait until the parents got home," Stevie admitted.

"My dad slapped me silly then they cried and made me get on my knees with them and pray for my salvation, you know, the same bullshit," Bobby said, rubbing his cheek.

"What about you?" Sylvia asked, looking over at me.

I didn't want to let on that I got beat.

"My dad was so cool. He thought that the lecture from the fireman and grounding me was good enough," I said as the stupid tears filled up my eyes. Nobody seemed to let on that they knew I was the stool pigeon.

We all agreed on one thing. None of us would talk about what we saw in that barn and that we were really sorry about it catching on fire and all. What a wild night it had been.

***

My mother would die soon of liver disease after that night and my father would get military orders to move at the end of the summer. We moved many more times before I grew up and lost track of Stevie, Sylvia, and Bobby. However, the memory of circling, chanting pig shadows and the barn that burned like an inferno traveled with me. I would always remember Old Man

Shotgun and the summer of '69.

I tried to look up Sylvia and the boys on Facebook but couldn't find them. I wished that I could put out a message asking, "If you see your name in this story, and you remember that night in 1969, the night of the swirling pigs, contact me." Just maybe we would share the memory and the desire to reach out to each other again. Just maybe. Who knows.

The Haunted Carpet

HA Grant

"Where's your husband, Melanie?" The detective placed a cup of coffee in front of me.

I shook my head. I'd been in the station for hours without anything to eat or drink, but I didn't touch the coffee. I knew it was a trick to make me trust them.

The detective's face hardened. "How come the window was broken?"

"I don't know," I lied, making a futile attempt to hide the red scratches on my hands. The late evening shadows closed in, bringing back terrible memories of the night before, but I didn't know how I would ever be able to explain them. The detective was never going to believe me.

The whole thing started when my husband Rick and I unlocked the front door of my late great-aunt Camille's townhouse in Washington, D.C. Aunt Cami had died and left everything to the two of us, including three floors of antiques and other priceless treasures she'd picked up over a lifetime in India and the Middle East.

Rick's stare grew more calculating as he moved into the house. Ignoring me as if I were the housekeeper, he pulled the drapes back from the parlor windows, letting the afternoon sunlight stream across the room. Green silk chairs. Tapestries. A vintage collection of wooden Moorish boxes and wall masks in a monstrous curio cabinet. Carved stone elephants with extravagant tusks stood by the fireplace.

Still ignoring me, my husband unfolded a copy of Aunt Cami's Last Will and Testament, scribbled some notes, and stuck his head in the dining room. We did a laborious walkthrough of the first two floors and finally ended up in the attic. It was crammed with more furniture and dusty trunks and boxes we were going to have to sort through, but the carpet stuck out because it was so large. It lay rolled up against the far wall.

"I didn't see that carpet in the Will," Rick said, rustling through the pages.

"She did say something about it, though." I stared at the carpet. Even in the shadows, you could see the fine workmanship. "It was one of her most prized possessions, but I wonder why she kept it up here."

"Let's get it downstairs and see what it looks like."

"It's really heavy," I said, wrestling with one end. "I can't possibly pick this up."

My husband rolled his eyes and hefted the carpet onto his shoulder. Expected me to be a lumberjack or something. He was a big guy, two hundred and forty pounds of meat and potatoes, while I'm barely a hundred and twenty counting my earrings.

"Got it," he grunted. "You just keep it from hitting the wall."

Somehow we half-hauled and half-dragged the carpet out of the dark attic down two flights of stairs into the parlor, which was the only room with enough floor space to roll it out. We shoved Aunt Cami's potted palms, her silk couch and chairs against the wall, and after a lot of huffing and puffing smoothed out the carpet.

It turned out to be enormous … and gorgeous. Drop your jaw and take your breath away magnificent. I don't know that much about oriental carpets, but I've seen a few in my life, and this beat every one of them. Fantastic birds and deer flew and leaped over a beautiful woven field, surrounded by persimmon, rose, and royal blue geometric patterns.

"Huh," Rick said in appreciation.

I brushed the dust off my hands. "Now I remember. It was a gift from a wealthy man in India who wanted to marry her. But I don't understand why she kept it in the attic."

"Because it's ruined. Look at the stain."

My heart fell. I'd assumed the stain was a shadow, but as soon as Rick pointed it out, I realized somebody had spilled something on the carpet. The stain had to be three feet across and resembled a knife. Somebody had probably done the dirty deed with a bottle of Bordeaux at a party.

"Right in the middle, too," Rick said.

"So I guess it really is ruined."

"Unless we can get it cleaned. We should get it appraised, find out what it's worth."

My husband disappeared into the kitchen, where his voice boomed out as he schmoozed somebody on the phone. "All settled," he said a few minutes later. He cracked his knuckles, one of his more annoying habits. "We've lucked out with a cancellation. The appraiser's coming at nine in the morning."

The rest of the day went by, nothing special, just me and my husband having some family togetherness. That's supposed to be a joke. Rick and I had been on the outs ever since he admitted to an affair I discovered when I went through his phone. The longest we'd spent together before this trip was in marriage counseling with some counselor with fluff for brains who didn't have a clue about how evil Rick could really be. Oh, and the woman he cheated on me with … that porky slut at his dealership. She was still calling the house.

That afternoon we went through Aunt Cami's papers and half the stuff on the first floor. Rick took notes about everything. Day one ended.

The next morning I crawled out of bed and pulled on my jeans and a sweater with one thing on my mind: hot coffee. Rick was snoring away with his nose hairs moving in the breeze. If the slut wanted him she could have him, as long as I got both houses. With a snicker, I crept downstairs toward the kitchen and took one quick look in the parlor.

The carpet was gone.

"Okay, Mr. Smartass, what's this about?" I blurted and turned on a lamp.

Sure enough, the carpet was gone. I couldn't believe it. The couch and chairs and potted palms were just where we'd shoved them against the walls, but the floor was completely bare. I even peeped behind the couch, thinking he'd probably rolled the carpet against the radiator, but it wasn't there.

Rick was still snoring away. It must have wiped him out to drag the carpet out of the parlor by himself. But why would he do that with the appraiser on the way? He couldn't be trying to steal it. I stared at the bare floor. It didn't make sense. Then I heard heavy footsteps. When I turned around, the oaf was looming over me with narrowed eyes.

"What's going on here?" he said. "What did you do with the carpet?"

"What did I do with the carpet?" I retorted. "Oh, that's a good one, Rick. That's priceless. What did you do with the carpet?"

"Me? The appraiser's almost here. Why'd you move it? Are you flaming nuts?"

"I didn't move anything. You moved it. I can't even lift that carpet. I only weigh a hundred and ten pounds."

"More like a hundred and sixty pounds. Melanie, Melanie, quite contrary. She's a liar. She can carry."

"What a wit," I told him. "Don't give up your day job. You'll starve to death."

I stomped upstairs with Rick behind me. The two of us were still going at it when we saw the open attic door. Rick reached over as if he were going to slam it shut when he gave me the coldest look I'd ever seen and then climbed the attic stairs.

The attic seemed to have twice as many shadows as before. There was the carpet, rolled up against the wall, exactly the way we first found it.

I clapped my hands. "Academy Award time, woo-woo."

Rick glared at me again. "I don't know how you did this by yourself, but this was a really dumb trick, Melanie."

"I'm not buying into your crazy games. You want the carpet that much, just say so. Are you planning on a divorce?"

"That's just what you'd like, isn't it, to be free of me. Well, you'll never get it." He gave me another nasty look, shouldered the carpet, and hauled it downstairs. Five minutes after he laid it out in the parlor, we heard a car door open and went to the window. A short, plump man with designer glasses and a too-tight black suit stepped out of a Lexus.

"Anthony Ferouk," the appraiser said when we met him at the door.

I shook his little manicured hand and let him inside. The tension lifted just to have him there. Shoes squeaking, Anthony Ferouk slowly walked around the carpet, staring at it. Maybe the carpet was worthless after all.

"Too bad about that spot," Rick said, hovering over him. "We figure somebody spilled a couple of drops of wine there. You think it's worth having it cleaned?"

"No, you don't want to do that," Anthony Ferouk said. "This could be a rare carpet. If this is the carpet I think it is, the stain has a special meaning."

"Oh, really? How rare?" Rick asked.

"Very rare, but I'd like a second opinion. Would you mind if I call the museum I'm affiliated with? They should be able to drive up tomorrow for a piece this important."

"And what's the special meaning of the stain?" Rick went on.

Anthony Ferouk gave us an odd smile. "I'd rather wait for my colleagues to examine it."

"Well," Rick said after he closed the door on the appraiser. "Well, well, well. A rare carpet. And somehow you found that out and tried to hide it for yourself."

"You're delusional," I said. "Just like you thought I loved you."

He laughed. "Well, at least Tanya loves me."

We didn't speak to each other the rest of the day. The sun went down. The moon rose over the streets of Washington and shone its spooky light through the windows. We sat in the parlor while the hours ticked toward midnight. I knew what he was doing. He was waiting for me to go to bed so he could steal the carpet. When the mantel clock chimed eleven-thirty, I couldn't help myself and yawned.

"We should turn in for the night," Rick announced.

"Be my guest," I told him.

"I'll follow you upstairs."

I smiled. "I'm going to stay here. I think I'll read Wikipedia, the whole thing."

Rick smiled back. "I think I'll read the U.S. Tax Code."

I stood up. "I've changed my mind. I'm going to turn in. But you know what? I'm going to sleep down here on the couch." By the time I ran upstairs and back with a blanket, my charming husband had pulled the couch into the middle of the carpet and plopped himself down.

"I'm sleeping here, too," he told me.

"And you can take a chair. I claimed the couch."

He yawned, gave me another evil smile, and stretched out with his filthy sneakers hanging over the arm of Aunt Cami's silk couch. I settled down in an armchair and pulled the blanket up to my chin. After a while lover boy began to snore, the same rhino snorts he'd kept up the whole night before. Unbelievable. That slut Tanya had really reeled one in.

I finally drifted off, don't ask me how. When I woke up, the room was dark and Rick was still snoring. The parlor was freezing. Shivering, I fumbled around for my blanket and realized it must have fallen on the carpet. When I reached down, my fingers touched the cold wood floor.

The carpet was gone again.

This time I wasn't fooling around. I grabbed Rick and shook him as hard as I could.

"Huh? Wha, wha, whatcha doin'?" he shouted.

"Where's the carpet, *sweetie*?" I punched him. "How'd you do it, *honey*?"

"What're you talking about?" He sat up, one eye shut and his hair sticking straight out.

I threw the front door open and stalked out to his Chevy Tahoe, but the carpet wasn't in the back. There was only one place he could have hidden it. By the time I stomped upstairs, he was right behind me, yelling and swearing. The attic was as black as night and had a malevolent feel that surrounded us like an ice-cold fist. And sure enough, there was the carpet, rolled up in the corner again.

"You did this," he said, red-faced with fury.

"I did not, you dirty cheater. I can't even lift the end. I only weigh a hundred pounds."

"More like a hundred and eighty pounds of lying lard."

"How did you get it off the floor when the furniture was on it?" I yelled.

By the time we stopped screaming at each other, hauled the carpet downstairs, and unrolled it in the parlor again, Anthony Ferouk and the museum experts were pulling up in a BMW. Anthony Ferouk wore another tight black suit. A man in a gray suit climbed out, followed by a washed-out woman in a perfect black dress who looked like she was in charge. They stared at the carpet in dead silence.

The woman shook hands with us. "Amanda Peele. You have a masterpiece."

"I never thought I would see this," the man in the gray suit added.

Anthony Ferouk nodded, soulfully pressing his hands together.

My husband cracked his knuckles, adding some class to the moment. "And what about the little spot?" he said. "Think we can get that baby out?"

"No," Amanda Peele said. "The stain is the proof that this is the Khaufnaak."

Rick laughed. "The what?"

Amanda Peele didn't laugh back. "The Khaufnaak, Hindi for Spooky, or the Haunted Carpet. The carpet comes with quite a tragic story. In the 15th century, the great Mughal emperor Shah Jahan buried his wife, Mumtaz Mahal, who died giving birth to their fourteenth child. Unable to accept her death, Shah Jahan grieved for two years. He wept until his hair turned gray. Finally, he built the magnificent Taj Mahal as a tomb to honor his beloved wife. Of course, the Taj Mahal is known the world over for its beauty and has become a symbol of the heart of India itself. Less known, though, is the strange story of this very carpet."

Here she gestured at the carpet we were standing on. "For centuries, this carpet adorned the Taj Mahal. One moonlit night, two turbaned princes surprised each other in the entryway. They had always been bitterly jealous of each other. The first prince, a short, heavy man, had rolled up the carpet and was hauling it down the steps, sweating with the effort. A third man, a carpet dealer from the city, was carrying the other end."

Rick and I stared at the carpet. I could have sworn it twitched.

Amanda Peele crossed her arms. "The second prince, a man with a black beard, demanded to know what they were doing.

'Taking what is mine,' the first prince said, sticking out his chin. 'I have consulted the oracles. I have proof that this is a magic carpet, and since I am a direct descendent of Shah Jahan I have taken what is rightfully mine and sold it.'

The second prince blocked the steps. 'A magic carpet?'

'Yes, it flies, according to all the signs, and rightfully belongs to me, so I have sold it. Now move out of the way.'

The second prince drew his knife. 'I am a direct descendent of Shah Jahan too so the carpet is rightfully mine.'

"Both princes drew their blades. As they began to fight over who owned the carpet, it unrolled down the steps of the Taj Mahal. Blades flashed. Royal robes flew as the princes dueled. Just as the first prince sliced his blade through the second prince's robes, the second prince plunged his knife into the first prince's chest, and there they died, grasping with their bloody fingers at the carpet they both claimed to own. Right there, right on that spot, in front of the carpet dealer, who was a witness." Amanda Peele pointed to the stain.

"Nice, a big fat bloodstain," Rick said, stepping back.

"So the carpet came to be named the Khaufnaak. Legend says the spirits of the two princes haunt the Khaufnaak to this day. Whenever anyone tries to sell the carpet, it rolls itself up and returns to its storage place."

"Ridiculous," Rick said. "And anyway, Aunt Camille bought the carpet."

"No, she didn't," I said. "I told you, it was a gift."

"You're sure this is the same one?" Rick asked.

"It has the famous stain," Amanda Peele said. "The stain would never come out. Made with Death's own hand, or so the story says."

Rick cleared his throat. "So what do you think this thing's worth?"

"Our museum would be interested in acquiring it, after we discuss it with the Board of Directors, of course, but we wouldn't be able to offer anything close to its true value."

"Which is what?" Rick said.

"Five million, perhaps," Amanda Peele said, looking at us carefully. "But perhaps you should also consider giving it to the museum as a gift."

Gift my eye. After they left, Rick disappeared into the kitchen, got on the phone, and emerged with a murderous smile. He began to roll up the carpet.

"And what exactly do you think you're doing?" I asked, hands on my hips. He pushed me out of the way. "Driving to Sotheby's in New York City."

"They'll come here, genius."

"Nah, I'm putting this ball in the end zone tonight."

"I want to remind you of one inconvenient little fact," I hissed. "That carpet is half mine. I own half of everything in this house, including that five million dollar stained rug."

"And I want to remind you of another inconvenient little fact," he said, leaning his beefy face close to mine. "Half that carpet is mine and I'm walking out the door with it tonight."

He threw the carpet in the Chevy and gunned the motor.

"Maniac," I yelled and jumped in without my shoes. We roared down the streets of Georgetown and over the Key Bridge. By the time we hit the Beltway, we were doing 90 mph and I was white-knuckling the seat.

"You're tailgating that g-g-guy," I said through my teeth.

Rick hunched over the steering wheel. "Five million big ones."

"You're gonna hit him."

"He gets a gold coffin."

I turned around. "I heard a thump in the back."

"We ran over something."

"There it goes again. It's the freaking carpet!"

"You want out, get out," he said.

I shut up and bit my nails and listened to the thumps. I don't even remember New Jersey. We barreled through the Lincoln Tunnel and shot through Manhattan in a stomach-flipping blur. My husband didn't take his foot off the gas until we collided with the curb in front of the Plaza Hotel. He wouldn't let anybody touch the carpet and hauled it through the lobby himself, grunting like a weight lifter. I ran after him in my socks, hoping nobody could tell we were together.

He finally unrolled the carpet in our suite. The place was gorgeous with gold-plated bathroom fixtures and a magnificent picture window across one whole wall. When I dared to look down, I could see the teeny little cars on Fifth Avenue crawling around Central Park.

"When does Sotheby's show up?" I asked him.

"In fifty-seven minutes," he said, cracking his knuckles.

We stepped on the carpet and smiled at each other.

"You should get dinner," I said. "We passed a hundred restaurants."

His hideous smile grew bigger. "There's a restaurant downstairs. Stay there all night."

"Come on," I said. "Hours in the car. Go take a walk."

"You take a walk. Me and room service, we're about to get intimately acquainted."

"You're not getting intimate with potato chips on a five-million dollar carpet."

He laughed and ordered dinner. When the steak and champagne arrived, he popped the cork and took a slug from the bottle.

"You're disgusting," I said. "You've been a pig our whole marriage."

He took another slug and stood over the stain. "This is it, Melanie. This is where it all comes together. We're going to sell this carpet and I get two-thirds. It was my idea to come up here and I did all the work."

I planted myself in front of him. "I don't think so, Rick. I get half."

"Too late, sweetheart. This train has left the station."

"We're not selling it at all, not without my okay."

"Oh, yes, we are. Five million dollars. You can take your third and I can give Tanya everything she's ever wanted."

Something moved under my feet. A ripple snaked through the carpet from end to end. At first I thought the floor was shaking, but the water glasses on the table were steady. Holding my breath, I stepped back as the carpet writhed again. The fringe rose a foot off the floor and snapped back down.

"Rick, get off," I said.

"In your dreams." He chugged the champagne.

The carpet rippled. It made a horrible flap. A monstrous ghost of a man with a black beard erupted out of the stain, winding and swirling toward the ceiling. His tormented eyes bulged and long jaws opened as he grasped a pale blade.

My mouth went dry. I hid behind a chair with my heart racing a thousand miles an hour. "Get off the carpet! Get off! It's a ghost!"

"Melanie sees the Easter Bunny. Melanie, Melanie wants that money."

"Get off the carpet, Rick!"

A second ghost crawled out of the knife-shaped stain, a pale fat prince with burning eyes. He seemed so angry that the veins protruded on his neck. His mouth formed a huge O as he tried to shriek, but no sound came out. I cowered down. The ghosts of the two princes circled each other in a terrible dance, pointing with transparent fingers. Their eyes rolled in their crumbling sockets and their rotting faces sagged. I could see the furniture through them. When one ghost swung his weapon at the other, the blade sliced through his smoky enemy.

The carpet began to roll up. When it moved under Rick's feet, he grabbed the fringe. The carpet bucked underneath him, but he held on.

The ghosts silently screamed at each other, mouths opening and closing. Their terrible pale hands gripped their blades as they swung and pierced each other all over again.

The carpet rolled up with horrible efficiency. Then it rose four feet from the floor with the ghosts writhing on top and Rick's body bulging in the middle with his fists sticking out.

"Rick, let go," I screamed. "*Let go!*"

"Five million dollars," he screamed back.

***

"So what happened then?" the detective asked. He'd finished his coffee an hour ago.

"The haunted carpet kept rising," I said. "And the ghosts kept trying to kill each other, and I could see Rick's fists grabbing the fringe at one end and his shoes poking out the other end. And then the carpet pointed at the window and smashed through the glass."

"Oh, it did, huh?" The detective's smirk grew wider.

I nodded. "The haunted carpet went right through the window like a ballistic missile. The glass sprayed everywhere in huge chunks. And then I ran to the windowsill and saw the carpet flying over Fifth Avenue, and the ghosts were still wrapped around each other, and Rick's shoes were still sticking out, and he kept screaming, "Five million dollars!" And the carpet sailed on like that into the distance, flying over Central Park into the night, until it got smaller and smaller and smaller and then … I couldn't see it anymore. They completely disappeared."

"So this one ghost fought the other ghost in the Plaza Hotel."

"That's what happened," I said.

The detective laughed. "You are one loony bird, Melanie. You're gonna tell me now what you did with your husband. You were really mad at him because he cheated on you, so you got even. You got more than even. You got him good. Did you cut him up in little pieces and stick him in your makeup drawer? Is he in a basement in the Bronx? In the back of his Chevy Tahoe? Where is he, Melanie? Where's your other half?"

I shook my head. "Flying south, rolled up in a rug."

The detective took the keys to the handcuffs and stood up with disgust. "You got anything else you want to say?"

"Just one thing," I said, taking a deep breath.

"And what's that?" the detective asked.

I met his eyes. "Will you check the attic one last time?"

About the Authors

AC Stone, KM Rockwood, BG House, and HA Grant are four Pennsylvania writers who have been telling stories for years. Contact them at www.Facebook.com at CafeFoulPlay or see their biographies for more ways to get in touch.

AC Stone (Ghosts of the Tsunami, The Wreck of U-913, and Swamp Mansion) was born, bred, and buttered in Baltimore, Maryland. He practices law in Westminster, Maryland and lives in Gettysburg, Pennsylvania. He writes spy novels, legal thrillers, and ghost stories. His hobbies include startling walruses as they sleep on rocky Canadian shorelines and nailing cubes of Jello to his office wall. He descends from a historic military family that first developed the use of the white flag, now an international standard. He once lost a debate with a cactus. Contact the author at andrew.stone@comcast.net.

KM Rockwood (Aunt Olga and the Werewolf, Escape from Hell, and Lure of the Owl) is the author of the Jesse Damon Crime Novel Series, published by Wildside Press. In addition to novels, she writes novellas and short stories. She draws on a varied background for her work, including working as a laborer in a steel fabrication plant and a fiberglass manufacturing facility. She has also worked supervising an inmate crew in a state prison, and has taught special education and GED in correctional facilities and alternative school. View her publications and read free stories at www.kmrockwood.com.

BG House (The Incident at Deep Lake, Buffalo Blonde, The Secret Life of Sam Dunlap, and Old Man Shotgun) lives with her husband and feisty black cat in Gettysburg, Pennsylvania. Her short stories have appeared in various anthologies. The Incident at Deep Lake is based on the author's short story titled "Albert Got Shot," which was originally published in 2011 and revised and printed here with the author's permission. Contact the author at bghhouse@aol.com.

HA Grant (Hell Couch, The Bad Thing, and The Haunted Carpet) is pursuing a degree in anthropology. She writes fiction when she isn't digging up old bones, hiking, or rescuing animals. Her science fiction books under the name Ann Grant include The Theory of Sam and Shadow Stations. Contact the author at anngrant717@gmail.com.